I0571570

Pleasure as a Higher Calling

Waking Up

Spicy Stories of Life, Love, Sensuality, and Lust

SAVANNAH ARIES

Pleasure Press

The events depicted in these stories are fictitious.
Any similarity to any person living or dead is coincidental.
The stories are merely a lush figment of the author's vivid imagination.

Second Printing 2017
Original copyright © 2011
Published in the United States of America by Pleasure Press

ISBN-13: 978-0615521657

This is dedicated
to the ones I've loved

Contents

Foreword

What Savannah Says About
the Little Indignities of Aging

Aging, with its not so subtle *little indignities*, requires courage and a healthy sense of irony. One of the more cruel aspects of this vexation is that although the years will show, you don't feel any differently than when you were younger. The spirit is eternal even as the body and mind ripen and begin to spoil. So even if you are able to avoid a mirror or a camera for any length of time, someone will be glad to provide you a reality check, whether you asked for it or not.

Consider women. A woman such as myself, for instance. A vital woman of a certain age. Still young at heart, still looks good, feels wonderful, is bright, engaging, sassy, juicy, energetic, independent, emotionally grounded, a woman who continues to desire and enjoy sex. What's the problem? There is no real problem, not at the moment. There are simply the *little indignities* to address each and every day.

"You look fabulous . . . *for your age.*"

"Wow! I'm surprised you can keep up the pace!"

"You sure don't act your age."

"Do you need some help with that?"

"I've always been curious about sex
with an older, more experienced woman."

These comments are the most benign sampling I've been subjected to in recent years. All were well meaning, none were malicious, each simply an aspect of the *little indignities* one must endure as one creeps toward advanced maturity. The *little indignities* require a vigilant sense of humor on perpetual duty.

Consider men. Men are not as mysterious as I once thought them to be. Still, an interesting, viable, engaging and, just as importantly, sexual man will always play an important role in my life. Otherwise, what could be his purpose at this point? Procreation? Men can't really be friends. They're resentful if you need them and more if you don't.

Younger men can stay with you sexually, but in general, they haven't yet gained experience or emotional maturity, so you wind up as their mentor. Older men, still interested in sex, can require adjustments or perhaps a pill, and most of the pleasure evaporates. If they have remained lively, they are on point and prowl for the younger woman. The rest, I'm saddened to say, are likely lazy, uninspired, and retired in every way, looking for a woman to take care of them, preferably, someone who can and will pay her own way as well as theirs.

Being awake, alive, and sexual myself, I understand and empathize with men exploring lusty adventures with younger lovers. The ravishing sex, the seductive sensuality of youth, is definitely all it's cracked up to be. There is, however, a *little indignity* that comes with such delectable desire in the heat of the moment with an ardent young lover. And that again is, since I don't feel any older than they are, I forget how my skin sags, that my face is lined and unevenly colored, or how bulges have appeared in places I never dreamed possible.

Thankfully, those *little indignities* are blessedly offset by the bonus of a passionate response which is longer, deeper, and more fulfilling than when I was younger. I wouldn't wish for a return to those times in my youth when many other things were more pressing, or mattered more, than expressing and enjoying my life, sensuality and sexuality. No longer exhaustedly task- or goal-oriented, now I am always oriented and receptive to whatever pleasure presents to me.

I am a mature woman in possession of a lusty desire and passion for life which continues to be attracting. Still the worst *little indignity* cannot be dismissed or overcome. The truth of my actual age, once revealed, is a psychological deterrent that trumps my accomplishments, charm, or sensuality. The early courtesans only survived into their twenties. I've thrived many more decades, but how long can this last?

This is the tragic relentless ticking of the biological clock younger women understand only as the time bomb of fertility. Unless one succumbs to losing one's mind, the true tragedy of that ticking clock is the loss of passion and desire for sex, which in my view is the greatest indignity and a point of no return for the aging body.

Making love often—having delicious sex, by the way—alleviates many of the *little indignities*. The pleasure of writing about it alleviates the rest.

The breeze at dawn has secrets to reveal.
Don't go back to sleep!
   ~ Rumi

Waking Up with Him

I had fallen asleep. I knew this was true because I had no interest whatsoever in men or sex. Since my divorce three years earlier, I had been this way most days. I could say I was content. I could say that I was relieved to not wake up with, contend with, deal with, or answer to anyone but myself. I could say that, but I missed my former spirited self. It isn't in my nature to live in a lull for long. Three years is a long lull for me, a woman of a certain age who has always reveled in adventures, mysteries, challenges and pleasures. Time was ripe for change.

One morning in early spring, as a sliver of hopeful sun peeked through the slit of my silky bedroom curtains, I luxuriated in the space between sleeping and awakening, stretching and contemplating the day. My mind mused; now would be an excellent time to wake up. The thought made me smile, a simple physical gesture. Encouraged, my body made a decision of its own and shivered in anticipation. I sensed my skin soften, my face lift, my organs rejuvenate, and most evocative: an arousal of my erotic sensory regions as they awakened and tingled, moistening with juicy sap, longing to experience and share pleasure.

How might I more lavishly experience my life? How might I live unguarded and carefree once again? That would be in direct contrast to the way I had trained myself to function these last difficult years. Life had been stressful and demanding, and little by little, I had erected barriers to shield myself from negative and undesired intrusions into my time and space, into my heart and psyche. Inadvertently, I had also jammed myself into a neutral gear emotionally and sensually.

What a sweet morning. I realized I no longer needed such vigilant psychic protection and began to dismantle those walls. I took a deep breath of appreciation for this awareness, dropped my shielding and shifted into forward. I touched my lusting body in celebration and recognized myself at once.

Days passed and happiness sprang out of seclusion, announcing its revival. Little things I'd been too busy or distracted to notice before began to amuse and entertain me. I relaxed into my sensuality and became more aware of colors, sounds, textures, scent and nuance. My days filled with pleasure and enjoyment. It was thrilling. And it was easy. Nothing outside of myself had changed at all. Yet once I changed my perspective, everything around me began to change as well.

I imagined my re-found passion would find a worthy cause on which to expend itself. A realm of possibilities expanded before me. I could start a new business or create the foundation I'd talked about for years. What about travel, or even moving to some exotic locale? I wasn't particularly thinking about men or falling in love but I was thinking about sex again. I was thinking about sex quite a lot.

My body began to yearn for sexual pleasures beyond what I was able to provide for myself, craving to be touched and explored by a man. A new man. I made no effort in this direction nor did I have any fantastic expectations. In fact, I couldn't even imagine how that might occur. Yet the appealing concept of sex, of making love again, began to crowd my awareness.

Then *he* appeared out of nowhere.

In a large crowded bookstore, I jockeyed for position in front of the long rack of best sellers, as I scanned for *The Audacity of Hope*, by Barack Obama. A guy behind me and I reached for it at the same moment and as I stood up, we collided, knocking each other off balance. He threw his arms around me out of instinct, steadied himself and me, then let go in the next instant.

"Ooops! I'm sorry. Here, take this one." I handed the book back to him while I grabbed the last one on the shelf.

"No problem. Hey, thanks," he said, brushing against my shoulder. I turned around, glancing up at him, nearly knocked off balance again by the impact of his presence. "I've been wanting to read this. Looks like you have too," he added.

"Yes, I have," I replied, pointing at the empty space on the shelf. "I guess we're not the only ones," He had an intensity, a surprising familiarity about him that I couldn't identify. Powerful, I thought to myself, and shivered. "This must be our lucky day. We got the last two copies."

"Yeah," he answered absently, glancing at the back cover. As if choreographed, we stepped out of the fray of other shoppers. He leaned closer, "Why are you so interested in reading this?"

"Well, probably like you, I was impressed when I first heard him speak at the convention. I was taken with his easy command. He seemed so genuine and earnest. I wanted to know more about him."

"Hmm, yeah, me too." He grinned, his eyes piercing into mine, arresting me for a second. His smile faded, became pensive, anchoring me. I held his gaze, but something shifted inside of me. I felt naked and vulnerable.

"Well, enjoy," I said, turning away, forcing my attention from him and toward my long list of things to do.

"Hey, thanks for scoring one for me," he called as I wandered off.

"My pleasure. Take care." I said, glancing at him over my shoulder. He smiled and nodded, turned and made his way through the crowd to the magazine section. Young, handsome, curious and likes to read. Nice, I mused as I rounded the corner to check on other books I'd ordered.

We found ourselves standing together again in the long check-out line. Laughing, we pointed at each other's book and formally introduced ourselves. We made our purchases at the same counter, chatting about the book and the phenomenon of Obama, then, like old friends, lingered at the exit.

"Hey, do you have time for a coffee, Ms. Savannah?" He beamed as we stood in the doorway. Something magnetic about him held me within his field. This gorgeous young man was flirting with me! His seductive grin seemed incongruent with his words: "We can talk about the world and who's gonna fix this mess we're in." He was laughing, but the energy behind his grin seemed fueled by something more edgy than an interest in politics. I wondered what was running through his mind.

I had plenty of errands to run but what came out of my mouth was, "I'd love to, Jackson. Why not?" Nothing on my list seemed so urgent now. I was flattered by his attention even if he was only interested in my opinions.

He ordered coffees and a sweet gooey scone. We settled into some soft upholstered chairs tucked in a far corner of the bookstore's crowded cafe. His attention made me feel hot and sexy. My still tanned skin and sun-streaked hair remained from a week in the desert last month and I was glad I had bothered with a little make-up before going out. I was even more grateful that I'd worn my tight jeans, creamy apricot sweater and knee-high boots. Nevertheless, I caught myself wondering how I must appear to him. He's young, many years younger than I. How many, I preferred not to think about at the moment.

"Aren't you gonna help me eat this thing?" He bit into the scone, licking his fingers. A smudge of caramel lingered on his luscious thick lips. My insides trembled when I imagined the tip of my tongue licking off that creamy smudge. An intangible magnetism seemed to inch our chairs closer and I shifted into high gear flirtation, engaging and entertaining him with vignettes and anecdotes. The book and politics forgotten, we laughed easily, enjoying each other's stories.

He claimed to be a superstar in sales. "I'm working my way to the top. I'll own the company someday," he said, with a boisterous laugh. "What do you do with yourself all day?"

"I'm a writer so I either have too much work and am overwhelmed with deadlines or not enough to keep me busy, like today. Wandering in a bookstore is not unusual; coffee with a strange but charming young man is."

He smiled, "You talk like you write stories. I bet you have lots of them."

"What makes you say so?" Was this meant as a compliment? I wasn't sure. "Everyone I meet has an interesting story," I added.

"You seem pretty comfortable and sure of yourself."

I didn't know how to respond. We sat in silence for a while assessing each other. He wasn't wearing a wedding ring, but I asked him if he had a family, any kids. He became more still and withdrew a bit, leaning back in his chair, his face unreadable. Here's a story, I told myself, but if he doesn't want to spill it to me, well, it's none of my business.

"Why do you ask? What about you?" He countered.

"Divorced. My kids are grown and have flown the coop," I said, realizing how natural it is for me to spill all. A slow smile spread over his face melting his serious expression. I startled myself by exclaiming, "Free at last! Thank God Almighty, I'm free at last!" erupting with laughter as I realized with relief how true this finally felt. He laughed with me and shook his head.

We chatted about our roots. His stemmed from the East Coast, mine from the South. Time evaporated until I focused on him and began to notice how his energy had changed. He was becoming more and more agitated as he glanced around the café. No longer was I his sole focus as before, and I became self-conscious, uncomfortable in his apparent discomfort.

"What's wrong, Jackson?"

"Look." He said, leaning toward me, his voice low and tinged with suspicion. He nodded toward the others sitting in the café. People seated casually at nearby tables had moved their chairs a little closer, blatantly eavesdropping, paying attention to us. This unnerved me. Until that moment I hadn't been aware of them at all, which is unlike me. I'm always curious about people around me, conscious of their energy.

He took my hand, insisting, "Let's go." He grabbed my arm, lifting me out of my chair and encircling my waist. He pulled me out of the store. "What happened in there?" He growled. "What the hell!"

"I don't know. Maybe those people were attracted to our positive energy and wanted to be included in the fun." I laughed lightly, but in fact, I knew it was true. "We're obviously having more fun than they are," I said, glancing back through the café warily. People were still staring at us. Well, we had generated some entertaining energy together, which in my experience never fails to attract attention. "Voyeurs!" I grumbled. "Weird for me not to not to notice. That bothers me. I guess you've captivated all my attention." Stuck in flirtation overdrive, I couldn't stop myself.

He stood like stone, his dark eyes again piercing mine, revealing nothing of his mind or feelings. So unlike me, I thought. I'm often told my pastel green eyes expose my every thought and emotion as they arise. Fatal in a game of poker. His look penetrated deeply not only into my eyes, but into the core of my body. I stood riveted in place—so close to him, so stirred up. His silence made me uneasy. What to do? Read this as a signal to say goodbye, I told myself. If only I could pry myself away.

"Well thanks, I had fun. Maybe we'll meet again one day," I said at last. Superficial. Stilted. Damn it. He said nothing. I hesitated, not wanting to leave as his silent gaze held me. I couldn't think what else to do. So much for his impression of me being comfortable and self-assured. With effort, I stepped away from his gravitational pull and turned toward my car.

"Hey, Savannah. Wait. Are you in a hurry?" He stepped behind me and took my arm again, pulling me close. "I'd like to talk with you some more, without an audience. Where's your car?" His wide grin returned and I couldn't take my eyes off his lips. My breath caught as I became aware his eyes were fixated on mine as well.

"Oh. Okay. I guess so. Why not?" My cheeks flushed and my pulse quickened as he followed me to my car, which I'd parked in the shade at the far end of the lot. The most disturbing and luscious feelings washed over me when I glanced back at him, so striking, tall and dark-skinned. Strong. Imposing. He appeared to be considering my ass and pleased with the view. Could that be true? Honestly?

As we settled into the car, I became conscious of a new chapter, a plot twist in my story, and I was feverish sitting so close to him. "Don't you think it odd the way we met today? Somehow you seem so familiar to me, as if we've met before, like I recognize you on some mysterious karmic or soul level," I rambled, horrified by my blurt. *Oh my God, Savannah. No!* The quizzical look on his face told me he did not share my experience. Why would I say such a thing? What is the matter with me? He made no comment but he leaned closer. I hoped the half grin on his face meant he was at least amused.

With my confidence frayed, I was on the verge of filling the space between us with nervous chatter when he asked, "What's going on here now? I can't seem to leave, even if I wanted to, which I don't. Who are you, Ms. Savannah? What's the deal with you?"

We sat, locked into each other's eyes, the few moments ticking by like eternity. "What do you mean?" *I knew exactly what he meant, but I'd already said more than enough.* "Why don't you tell me what's going on? Who are you and why are we sitting in my car?"

In slow motion, we leaned into the space between us as if mesmerized. He bent forward, his lips, soft, inquisitive, electric, kissing mine. He pulled back a little, his eyes lingering on my lips, perhaps gauging my reaction, my receptivity. *Oh! I'm receptive alright, with no restraint or inclination to consider what the hell I'm doing with this beautiful stranger.* With his hand cradling the back of my neck, his attention remained on my lips torturing me with anticipation. He seemed to relish the sultry tension until at last he took my face in his hands and devoured me. I surrendered without a thought.

His touch generated shocking sensations, swirls of vivid feelings and images, somehow familiar like a neutron blast of *deja vu* shot straight into my core. My world tilted, my axis shifted. My cells lit up, my nerves vibrated. We kissed. Wordless. His hands caressed my cheek, his fingers entangled in my fine blonde waves, mine twisting his soft dark curls.

"I want to see you again," he whispered. "I need to. Can we do that?" With his intensity so explicit—so sexual—I was thrown off guard. To say I was vulnerable, out of my depth, unable to move, had just experienced a psychedelic event horizon, wouldn't come close to describing how I felt. I didn't have to think twice about wanting to see him again. I couldn't think at all. My body was doing all the thinking. The only thought registering in my dazed mind was yes. Yes, we can do that. We relaxed back in our seats again. He shook his head from side to side, as if perplexed or bemused. I involuntarily mirrored his gesture, for my part, more than perplexed. Bewildered.

"What?" I asked him, uneasily. He sat there staring at me; his intense energy felt directed into my soul. What were his thoughts, what did he want? He shook his head again and shrugged his shoulders but said nothing, a grin spreading across his face. What I wanted came into clear focus for me. Those lips! I wanted those lips pressed against mine again.

We exchanged numbers. "I'll call you," he said. A promise? I hoped so but I couldn't speak. The back of his hand brushed my cheek lightly, almost affectionately. He eased himself out of my car. With his back to me, I was taken with the powerful, purposeful way he sauntered to his car. When he opened the door and turned to face me, with his arms crossed over his broad chest, he flashed that disarming grin, again shaking his head. He lingered before finally sliding into his car and turning the ignition. A silent giggle buried deep within me threatened to spill into wild laughter. He waved, then drove off. My laughter erupted into hilarity.

I sat frozen in place yet on fire, grinning from the inside out, and now I shook my head again too, in disbelief. What kind of auspicious event just transpired here? Encounters like this are the stuff of movies and romance novels. I'm sitting in my car in a bookstore parking lot with a faint taste of caramel on my tongue.

What had possessed me to meet, then kiss, and now imagine more than that with this guy all within the stretch of little more than an hour? Oh my God! I trembled with surprise and anticipation. As I pulled into traffic, I made a decision. No matter what else transpired, I intended to enjoy every moment of this magical encounter.

And he did call me. He called and we talked on the phone every few days for the next couple of weeks, but we made no plans to meet. We flirted, dancing around the unspoken issue of what came next. I made a solemn pact with myself not to initiate anything further, although I longed for him to, and could think of nothing else. I reminded myself daily: do not try to figure it all out, analyze or decide anything about him. Absolutely do not try to orchestrate or make anything happen. I wanted to experience whatever unfolded without expectation and without manipulating any particular outcome. That became my mantra. In theory.

In actuality, I desperately wanted to spend some intimate time with him, touch him, kiss him, make love with him. So I did my best with my theoretical agenda, even though not taking action is unnatural for me. I did not act on any of the passionate scenarios of us together that I conjured in my imagination. I did compile an impressive list of possibilities should he decide to make any of them happen. But I would have to wait for him to act.

When he called me, an undeniable sexual tension underscored our every conversation. He'd ask me to tell him about my room, or what I'd had for breakfast. He'd want to hear what I was wearing, which I would then describe in detail, down to the lace of my bra and silkiness of my panties. Once I called him from my bath, teasing him about how luxurious and sensual I felt soaking in the warm scented water imagining him watching me. He released a deep low groan and told me how he pictured me lying with my head back, eyes closed, knees spread, touching myself. He nailed it.

The unspoken desire between us grew and became even more palpable in the long pauses within our conversations. I began to understand his confusion, his resistance to connecting and allowing himself to get closer to me. He admitted he had strong feelings he couldn't explain. I inherently knew what he didn't say. Never had he expected to be attracted to someone like me. He struggled with that fact. The same struggle applied to me though nothing could top my intrigue and excitement.

Still, we were compelled to move toward each other rather than away. We seemed to have no choice. Even though our differences encompassed more than gender, age or race, we were compelled. I learned more about the chasms between our perspectives, experiences, education, culture, style, and approach to life. Even our astrological signs opposed each other. I didn't care about any of those things in regard to him. I couldn't be sure what he cared about.

I knew his life was full and meeting me may have been an intrusion, perhaps delightful, but not the serendipitous adventure it had become for me. I suspected he had another life, perhaps a girlfriend or even a wife and family. When we met at the bookstore he had skirted the subject, but he also hadn't denied it. I had a strong sense, but I wanted to be wrong so I ignored my intuition. We hadn't connected again and might never, so what did any of that matter?

"Hey, how's your morning? I had some time to read the book last night. What do you think so far? Not exactly what I expected." He asked me this calling from his car on his way to work one morning.

The book? Not at all what I wanted to talk about. I'd just awakened from another delicious dream of him and was making coffee, savoring the lingering lust still tingling in my body. I exerted a strong effort to shift gears. "Well he's brilliant, isn't he? So brilliant I wonder if I'm actually grasping the discussion, so much about constitutional law, definitely a scholar." I laughed, because at the moment I couldn't care less about the constitution, history, politics, or anything but him.

I had a one-track mind concerning Jackson. Still, I vowed to keep to my agenda. But the truth was I wanted him. I wanted to kiss him again. I wanted him to touch me. These thoughts were always on my mind, the playground that made my juices surge and my heart race.

Later in the afternoon he surprised me, calling again. "Hey, what are you doing right now? Want to meet me for a drink?"

"Sure. Where?" A warm impulse spread through my entire being. He was relenting.

"Well, I had in mind that new place not far from you, but sitting in a crowd attracting weird attention again isn't what I want right now. I want to see your smile and spend some time with you. Alone." A long pause before he chuckled, "How about it, Savannah?"

Another long pause—should I invite him to my house? My tummy fluttered at the thought. "Sounds fine by me. What and when, and I guess where, did you have in mind?" I was thrilled, and a wreck.

"I was hoping you'd ask me to your place and I was thinking, how about now?"

"My place?" My one-track mind tripped its safety switch. "Of course, you're invited to my place. Come soon." Did I just say come soon? I could come right now with the thought of his arms around me, his lips.

"Just need your coordinates and I'm on my way."

Coordinates? I gave him the address and we hung up. Oh my God! He's coming here? Soon? I made a sweeping pick-up of my home, took a quick shower and sifted madly through my armoire for the best thing to wear, deciding finally on my soft blue silk Chinese lounging pajamas. I wear them often; the pale blue is right for me and they're comfortable and sensuous. I stared at my reflection in my dresser mirror. What message does this image send? Should I change, wear something less, well, provocative? The sleeves and pants are long and cover my entire body, but the way the silk drapes reveals my shape and obvious nudity beneath. I caught sight of my bed behind me and sighed. I'd forgotten to breathe again.

I couldn't calm myself. I paced the house like a nervous cougar. The sudden realization that I was on the verge of becoming one was so funny to me. I laughed out loud at the scandalous thought. I ought to be more scandalized by the idea of becoming a cliché. Then the bell rang. I froze in momentary shock. Destiny had arrived at my door. I took a deep breath and opened my home to him.

"Wow!" he exclaimed in a long low exhale. He set a bottle of Malbec on the kitchen counter and stood in front of me, his arms crossed over his chest, his intense gaze unreadable. Until this moment the fact that we'd only flirted on the phone hadn't entered my mind. My knowledge of him was based on intuition and fantasy. We didn't know each other. This was only the second time we'd met in person and I'd not only opened my home to him, I was standing near him naked beneath this silk.

My heart raced in a moment of panic and I stepped back. He reached for me, catching me at my waist, pulling me into his arms, kissing my forehead. He shook his head from side to side, smiling in the way I had remembered, before resting his hands on my fluttering heart. His fingers stretched across my chest. For a moment he acted almost shy.

"You're nervous. Me too, I guess," he whispered, placing one of my hands on his heart, lightly kissing my neck. His heart was racing in tandem with mine. I could scarcely catch my breath, let alone speak. His nervousness assured me, calming me in a strange way. "Don't be," he said, cupping my chin in his other hand. He kissed my lips, lingering, before standing back and looking me over. His grin returned. The way he bit his lip and shook his head was not only familiar but endearing to me. His command and confidence returned. I became giddy. The moment I'd longed for had arrived.

"You look beautiful and mmm ... you smell mmm ... " His voice trailed off in a sensuous whisper. He pulled me close again and leaned into my neck, slid his hands from my waist up my back over the smooth silk and finally through my hair. My body couldn't resist his magnetic pull. I searched his eyes for some clue to help me understand what to expect. He glanced past me, taking in the next room. Pulling me along with him he began to wander slowly through the house. "I wondered what your place would be like. I see now it's a lot like you: cheerful, warm and comfortable. Kinda different. How would you describe your, uh, decorating style?"

"Eclectic?" I couldn't think what else to say.

"Eclectic, huh? Yeah, that's it. Nothing definite. Lots of everything." He laughed, turning to me, pulling me close to him again, nuzzling my neck, intoxicating me with his embrace, our bodies pressed close.

I wanted him to experience warmth and comfort with me. I wanted him welcomed in my home. I wanted him to stay. I wanted him period. He loosened his hold again and began to wander from room to room, inspecting the locks on every door. I trailed along behind him.

"What are you doing?" I asked. Why did he think he needed to check the security of my home? Whose safety was he concerned about? Mine, or his? Why was I following at his heels like a puppy?

"Habit," was his only explanation. He stopped abruptly at the open door to my bedroom and I rammed into his back. He reached for my hand and I stood behind him while he peered inside. I wondered what caught his eye, what he might be thinking, what he felt. I tried in vain to gain control over what I was thinking and feeling as his eyes probed my most intimate personal space. My heart began to race again.

He turned to me, enfolding me in his strong arms, melting me with his warmth, a genuine tenderness I hadn't experienced nor expected from him. But when we kissed this time, a charge of voltage passed between us and electrified me. My circuits overloaded and began to melt down when his stiff cock pressed against me.

I reached for him, standing on my toes, pressing my body as close to him as possible. I kissed him, waking up from my daze, unable to contain myself, ravenous, my nipples hardening against his chest as they glided against the silky tunic between us.

Anything else was forgotten as we held each other at the threshold of my bedroom. He clasped my hand and led me in, pausing before the dresser mirror, where I had stood in anxious anticipation, just a few minutes ago. My room looked different now, the light dimmed as if candles had been lit. We faced each other, silent, transfixed, so close heat radiated between us though we weren't quite touching. Time paused, then noticing that we'd stepped out of it, made a quiet retreat.

Jackson slowly unfastened the first clasp of my silk top, kissing my lips and throat. I felt faint. His face close to mine, his lips a hair's breadth away, he opened the next clasp and cupped both breasts, bending to glide his lips onto my nipples. My knees threatened to give way. He pulled the last clasp apart, slipping the silk from my body, holding me at my waist as it drifted in slow motion to the floor.

His dark eyes, so mysterious, stared into mine, while he slid his hands through the waist of my loose silk trousers. One hand glided over my behind, caressing my naked cheek, the other wandered down my belly and hesitated. The tenderness of his touch melted me. The palm of his hand tentatively covered my mound, our gaze fused. His fingers slid into my moist throbbing secret. He touched me there. My body and mind became acutely aware and responsive to every languid change in his posture and pressure, his sultry eyes, the touch of his hands on my shivering skin, his musky intoxicating scent, the thrill of his exploring fingers. Jackson, in my room, making love to me just as I'd dreamed. Surreal.

"Mmmm. Savannah. So smooth, so mmmmm ..." his whisper faded into my hair.

The late September sun was setting. The slanted filtered light seeping through the creamy sheers on my bedroom windows cast a single golden ray across my bed. A warm hue filled my room. Never had it seemed so inviting. And I felt weightless as if gravity had deserted me.

The blown glass vase on my bedside table, filled with slender pink calla lilies,, captured my attention for a moment, orienting me back into my body. I reached up to steady myself, clutching the sculptured muscles of his shoulders. He unfastened the one clasp holding up my pants, his breath catching as they slid down my legs to the floor, his gaze shifting slowly from my eyes down my body to the lush pool of blue silk that lay at our feet. He stood back from me then, shaking his head in that way he does, his smile disrobing even my nakedness. I closed my eyes.

He whispered, "You scare me—you're so beautiful right now, so soft, so vulnerable, so tempting. Yeah, you're a temptation I can't resist." His hands gently slid over my back and thighs while he kissed my checks and eyelids. "Open your eyes, Savannah. Look at me." I did as he asked and got lost in him. "God, you're so sensual." He stared into my eyes again, consuming me with his power, confessing in a low whisper, "Your eyes. And lips. I haven't been able to get the memory of your lips off my mind for two weeks, imagining how they would feel on my body. I want your mouth all over my body." He guided me backwards to the bed, pulled back the comforter and laid me down, opening my thighs just enough to witness me, my desire exposed to him. "Damn. You are so sexual, so un-selfconscious, just the way I knew you'd be."

Un-selfconscious? I was completely conscious of every particle of myself, of him, his attention on me. I had become electrified, a superconductor conscious of every breath, every word he uttered, every sensation in my body. I was insanely conscious of the way his hands moved over my flesh. How my flesh shimmered from his touch. Enflamed by the desire I saw in his eyes. How it matched mine.

He peeled off his clothes and overwhelmed me further. His gorgeous toned muscles and aroused body, tall and dark. His mouth, those thick lips I had been longing to kiss. He stood before me erect, hung like a stallion. Oh God. I held out my arms to him as he breached the space between us in one step and pressed himself against me. Oh my God.

He touched me. His touch awakened a forgotten passion buried deeply within both my psyche and my body. He ignited my deepest sexual yearning. My nature understood this, my body remembered and responded. When he entered me, I was ready, certain he was the one I could open myself to receive.

He lowered himself over me, penetrating me in slow motion. His intense dark eyes stayed fixed on mine. Lifetimes of pleasure released in waves, and I was convinced I remembered him this way from another time and place. The way we fit and moved together was so natural, so attuned. Immediate. He made love to me, with me, kissing my lips and cheeks, slipping down the sensitive curve of my neck to devour my breasts. I melded to him as if we were made for each other, undulating in fluid sync, in luscious matched rhythms.

We escalated. Our desire became urgent. I clung to him. He slowed his thrust. "Please. Oh, please don't stop," I begged. I craved him. He peered into my eyes again smiling. He kissed my open mouth. His wide hands reached under and lifted my hips. He plunged deep within me. I arched my back moaning with pleasure. He reached the end of his control, surging in feverish anticipation of our coming communal climax. Jackson exploded inside of me, groaning from his depths, pumping his seed into my creamy reception. I imploded, peaking with him in waves of ecstatic rapture. The world I'd known before shattered in a million fractured shards of light and sound. He opened me and he filled me. Our hearts pounded in unison as he lay on top of me, his hands tangled in my hair, his lips and breath buried in my neck. Held tight in his embrace, I could no longer differentiate our edges, where his skin blurred into mine. This is how it started with us.

That night he became a living, breathing part of me, permeating my thoughts and dreams, penetrating my heart, my mind, my body. Over time, I would struggle with the heady imbalance of this intersection with the rest of my life, especially as I learned more about his. If I remembered my covenant to be present in the moment, I was able to let it all be and enjoy our reunion. Reunion is what I called this precipitous happening. The sensations, pleasures and even the confusion he would bring me were worth it, come what may. And oh God, I would come and come again.

Late the next afternoon he called, divulging in one steady stream of exclamations, "Damn, Savannah, I couldn't stop thinking about you all day. I pictured your body, every inch of you emblazed in my mind like the negative from a photo. I've been thinking about fucking you every second since I left last night. The way you taste and smell, the way you kiss me. I'm going crazy thinking about you. And when you look at me like you do? Like you know me so well, even though there's no way you could? Like I matter, like I'm important in some weird way. I asked you this once already, now I'm asking again. What the hell is this? What's happening? What's the deal with you?"

I had to think for a minute. I wasn't sure what was happening and I had no idea what would ultimately happen with us. I was barely able to contain the enormity of my feelings about him. I heard myself say, as if from a dream, "This is what you mean to me. I see you. I recognize you. I appreciate you for your heart and mind and, well, now your delicious sexuality. I crave the way you make me feel. A fire started and I don't want to think about what this means. Thinking doesn't help. That's all I know."

Speaking with such passion startled me and caused a sudden uneasiness within me. I sensed there was more, maybe much more than I'd bargained for. As for now? I was game. I realized I was in, no matter the direction we took.

"I want to stay with you tonight. Please." He pleaded.

"Yes, please, I want you to. When can you come?" He wants to stay with me. I want this as well, don't I? Yes. Absolutely. My uneasy intuition short-circuited and sank in the depth of my desire. "Hurry. Because I can't stop. Coming that is."

He laughed. "You're funny. You're sexy and beautiful and funny and your honesty turns me on so much I can't concentrate on anything else. I'm on my way."

I hadn't expected him and had just been preparing a simple pasta and salad for dinner. He came through the door, drawing me into his arms like a magnet. I flung my arms around his neck and kissed him as though he'd been gone for lifetimes. All the desire and yearning from the previous night flooded into the kitchen in a shocking tsunami of emotion. He held me almost too tight for a moment, then pulled back and gazed into my eyes. Pensive. He does that. Searching. What was he looking for? He offered nothing of his deeper thoughts. Maddening. I reminded myself that he was young, and a guy. Though in my experience, young or any age, that trait in a man rarely varies.

The aroma of garlic and basil sautéing in rich olive oil caught his attention.

"Mmmmm. Damn. What're you cooking?" He licked his lips and loosened his hold on me.

"Hungry?" Was he ravenous, like me? I shivered with the prospects of him as dessert and left his arms to open the wine still sitting on the counter from last night.

"Oh, yeah, I'm hungry, but let's eat this first." He chuckled and leaned over the stove, savoring the dish with a deep inhale. Delighted at how he was enjoying himself, I caught his eye and winked. He straightened himself and smiled, licking his lip again. It felt easy and familiar to have him here, which pleased me.

I set him a place at the table across from mine and poured the wine. The next moment jarred me out of my reverie. My cozy feeling of familiarity collided with a memory of me serving this same dinner to one of my teenage sons not too many years ago. I hadn't allowed myself to address the disparity in our ages before this. Obviously, I'm much older than he. But how much older? Decades? God. Did the same thoughts about me concern him? Could his frame of reference encompass how much older I am?

He performed a quick inspection of the house, as before, without my shadow. I lit a candle, clicked on some soft dinner music, and filled his plate. He returned, sat down and reached for my hand.

"Would you like to say the blessing?" I asked.

"You've made this a blessing. Thanks for all this," he answered.

I couldn't take my eyes off him. He ate with enthusiasm and filled another plate. I had a lump of years stuck in my throat. A sip of wine didn't make it go away. I took a swig and swallowed that lump, for the moment. I'd have to find a way to keep it from choking me.

"Real good. Great. Hmmm. So she cooks, too." We sat and held each other's gaze, me studying his expression, his skin, his lips. At last he stood, flashed his disarming grin and shook his head as if in disbelief. He took my hand again, and scooped up the plates with his other, unloading them with a clatter on the counter. He pulled me close, lifted my chin and kissed me. His lips slipped down the curve of my neck, his tongue seeking the moist crevice between my breasts as he stepped us toward the bedroom. My downward spiraling emotions evaporated, enticed by the obvious desire straining against his jeans.

We stood just as we had the night before, but now our eyes locked in pure lust. Grins of anticipation, breath held in suspended animation. He grabbed my waist, his powerful hands grasping the small of my back, pressing his ramrod cock against me. I shoved my hands down his jeans, clutched his ass, and ground myself into him. He ripped off my jeans and shirt and threw them across the room. I stripped off his clothes in a crazed pursuit of flesh. He grasped my wrists and held them behind my back, licking my breasts. I dropped to my knees. My tongue slid down his torso to the tip of his cock. My open mouth sucked him in. He stilled himself in the pleasure for a moment before yanking me back up and tossing me onto the bed. We fell onto each other like animals, panting, moaning, and sweating, tumbling in frenzy from one position into another. Tonight he was overcome with rowdy lust and the urgent satisfaction of it. Me too!

He climbed over the top of me and slid inside my ready slickness, his tongue slithering out of the corner of his mouth, lapping my breasts and neck. He dipped into my shallows then plunged to the depths. I held on, an immediate pressure building, a rumbling force set in motion, yearning to erupt. He rolled over onto his back without disengaging, pulling me with him. I positioned myself into place on top of him, his charged engorged cock pressed against both my cervix and spot. My entire body quaked in seismic upheaval. I came. Came apart at the seams. I rode him through the aftershocks until the earth stopped shaking. He pulled my face to his and kissed me back into this world.

We rolled over again, still engaged like spoons. He dipped in and out from behind, grasping my hips, holding us together.

Up on his knees then, mounting me from the rear, he lifted me into place beneath him whooping and hollering, driving himself into me. I came again in ecstasy when he spewed everything he had into me, pumping until he exhausted himself, shouting my name into the back of my neck. His body wrapped around me, touching every delirious inch of me inside and out. We never separated. Collapsing together, he rolled onto his side and held me, one arm under my breasts the other over my mound. Our bodies curved, fastened together, him soft now yet still filling me. I trembled with gentle spasms, aftershocks of little orgasms continuing to come in waves until we both drifted into sleep.

Our first entire night together began with primal fierceness and we fucked until obliterated. Later, in the middle of the night, we woke up and rolled into each other again and made slow luscious love. Sharing ourselves with tenderness, confessing tiny secrets, we coasted into orgasm together. We held one another in dreamy slumber till dawn. Once in the early morning, I awakened as he mumbled my name and nuzzled closer into me. I began to understand that he cared for me, that his interest was more than curiosity. I gazed at him sleeping in such peace and sensed something had awakened in him as well, something he hadn't expected or prepared for.

I was awake. My body enlivened, my spirit enriched. *I woke up.* I didn't want to sleep, even as he did. I spent the early morning hours memorizing him until the warmth of his arms and quiet rhythm of his breath lulled me back into his deep reverie once again.

"Oh my God! I gotta get going," he growled at the clock squinting at the sun peeking through the windows, jarring us out of our tangled slumber. "Damn! I'm already late. Don't get up, baby. I'll call you later."

He showered and quickly dressed, throwing me a kiss from the door as he rushed out. I lay in bed wishing for nothing more than to extend this heaven, this utter contentment forever. His scent on the pillows and sheets induced my vow to never wash them again. My body was saturated with him, his cum sticky on the inside of my thighs. I vowed never to shower again. His essence, his seed resting deep inside of me was home, I wanted to hold onto it for as long as possible. I wanted him back, lying beside me. I'll never forget how satisfied, how complete my fulfillment was that gorgeous morning.

For many months we reveled often in lust and love. He couldn't always stay over and sometimes he wouldn't come at all for a week or more. Whenever that was the case, I lived in anticipation, sometimes distress, wallowing in self-doubt and recrimination. If several days went by with no contact, I'd find some reason to initiate it. Eventually I had to acknowledge that without my insistence—sometimes gentle, other times dramatic—we would have spent much less time together.

Sometimes, when I called, he would seem distant, unavailable, too busy to talk. He would make a quick excuse to disconnect. I became ruefully clear about two things. First, he had all the power and dictated the terms of our engagement. Second, I had abandoned my own agenda, willing to be at his beckoning when it suited him. Both of these realizations humiliated me. Even so, I convinced myself important lessons were being learned, but exactly what those lessons were eluded me. When red flags were raised, I managed to either pull them down or turn them pink. My friends had to admit I'd become more lively, energized, and youthful. They also told me I was pathetic as hell.

Ah, but when we spent time alone together we meshed, unable to keep our hands and mouths from touching, exploring each other. Those early excursions into our steamy sexuality were an erotic, aerobic, physical, and emotional workout. I began to develop a philosophy incorporating daily acts of conscious sensuality into my spiritual practice. All acts of pleasure became my worship. I hadn't known I could come so undone with desire. Time passed and he proved to be quite skilled at undoing me.

A critical component of this story, one I'm forced to ac-knowledge about myself, was the way my chemistry, curiosity, and hormones won out over logic. All along they won out over my best interests, rationalizations, and discernment. They even out-willed my free will. Whenever I stood back and reviewed the dichotomy of our unlikely union, I had to admit what my friends noticed was true. I was revived and renewed. He did make me feel fresh, young, and alive. That I also felt silly and ridiculous made me laugh. I had never experienced so many luscious and wrenching emotions all in the same context.

I didn't care then and I don't care now. I made the choice upon my awakening, even before we met, that I would smear my palette with all the colors: intense and pastel, blended and in contrast, pleasing and yes, even conflicted. I wanted to savor them all. Waking up with him made my life more vivid and alive with every intense emotion. I could say I allowed this story to unfold as a gift of discovery to myself. Our strange magnetic at-traction confused us. At times, we became conflicted with both the powerful draw towards and the strong need to pull away. But I'm also enamored by adventure and Jackson was a wild ride in many delicious and agonizing ways.

The only thing I can say with any certainty is that he was the impetus for my sexual re-blooming and healing, the wake-up call for my passion. He triggered my orgasmic complexity and supplied the youth juice I absorbed into my DNA with reckless abandon, casting a backward spin on my biological clock. I am quite certain that making love with him—our galvanic sex— was the reason my body cycled out of menopause and back into a lusty regeneration. For his role in this miracle, I still cherish him.

For him the story was something much different. He strug-gled with the parts of his life he'd been unwilling to share with me: the secret I'd been unwilling to press him to address. Eventually he confessed to young children and an estranged wife, with whom he claimed he wanted to reconcile. At that point the armada of red flags pierced my heart as they dropped anchor. I wanted to jump ship. I couldn't. I expected him to do so. He didn't. The ambiguous way he managed his conflict spoke volumes to me about him as a man. His youth and inexperience, values, integrity and cultural conditioning were all on the line.

I also struggled, because I had no easy explanation for the fact that he consumed my thoughts and there was nothing I could do about it. We could never be in a conventional relationship, ever. So why I would sink into a wretched melancholy when I admitted this to myself made no sense. He would never be the one, not this time, not in this lifetime. And this is where the mystery had me captured. Our inexplicable link compelled me to believe we had been joined as one in other lifetimes. An esoteric concept as real to me as it was ridiculous to him rendered the situation truly hopeless. Yes, I was pathetic.

And yet, a fabulous freedom existed for me in all the angst. I was free to express my authentic self with as much passion as I cared to. I had nothing to lose since I knew I would surely lose him at some point. I didn't need 20/20 vision to see the ultimate destination. When we would arrive, I'd leave up to him.

One dreary day, *when* became now. "We need to talk," he said, calling from work one afternoon. Each word a hesitation, the tone and tension of his voice alerted me. "I'm on my way over."

Anxious, I waited for him to arrive at the door. We stood facing each other, uneasy in the dim light of the kitchen. I reached for him but he took only my hand, shaking his head the way he does. He stood, his shoulders tense, his expression solemn, no sign of his usual amusement or humor. Time froze and so did I, the silence and tension dropping into a chasm between us.

"Just listen to me, please," he began tentatively. "How can I explain this to you? I've tried before. Probably won't come out right this time either, not the way I mean anyway. But please, just listen, and hear me out for once."

"Haven't you always had your say, done as you pleased? God! Haven't I always acquiesced?"

"Yes and no. Something about you keeps a hold on me. I don't know why or how you do it or even what it is." He struggled to hide his discomfort and control his emotions before continuing. "I care about you. You know that."

"How can that be true? You're doing this again."

"This thing with us doesn't work. If sex were the only issue, it wouldn't be such a problem. But I fucking can't stay away from you for any length of time. I've never understood it, never been able to get a grip on it and that's the problem. You take up too much space in my thoughts. How can I move on with you still in my life? I told you from the beginning I couldn't get too connected to you. People need me. I have things to do." He looked away from me. I imagined I saw a tear threatening to escape his eye; one was leaking from mine. "I have things I need to accomplish," he continued as if rehearsed. "I can't do this anymore."

I didn't feel like being easy on him. I had in the past. He'd said these same things to me several times before. He would stay away for a couple of weeks, sometimes even months. No matter what either one of us did, or who else we spent time with, we'd fall in together again. I can't say what I expected from him or myself. I didn't have the luxury of expectations with him. Each time we came back together rendered another rip in the fabric of what we'd had before, though we'd both attempted to mend it.

I had wanted to hold myself open—hold my heart open—but certainly hadn't anticipated having it ripped open. I had wanted to delve deeper. I had wanted to experience a more profound sexuality. I had. The experiment absorbed me—hooked me—but he would always pull himself back, out of reach.

I fabricated and embellished our delicious story as a fantasy of star-crossed lovers. Even though this affair had begun as curiosity and entertainment for me, I soon found myself on a steep and difficult learning curve, sometimes fascinating, and other times wretched. Maybe learning to traverse that slippery curve was the sole purpose of our complicated destiny. I don't believe he realizes even now it was a miracle we met in the first place.

"Aren't you going to say anything?" He pleaded. I observed my attention spiraling downward, sinking into the divide growing deeper and wider between us. He lifted my chin and forced me to look at his face, into his eyes.

"What do you want me to say?" I asked pulling away, not willing to allow him such intimacy. "What can I say this time to make any difference?" I struggled to remain as cool and detached as possible—an act of sheer will, but only an act.

"How can we keep this going? We could never give each other what we really want or need. You know that's true," he continued, allowing me to witness his misery.

With that my own misery welled up, ready to spill into his. I couldn't be angry. I couldn't even be too upset, thrashing right up to the edge of this chasm before, as we had. But now my emotions made me weak. I didn't want him to see me cry. He fought with his own emotions, doing a much better job of overcoming them than I. I understood that his main conflict was finding the words to end this story right, which meant, of course, right for him.

"Why are you quiet now? You've never been at a loss for words. Where's your usual damn philosophy lesson? What? No sassy attitude?" As he baited me, I held back the tears threatening to drown me. "Goddamn it, Savannah. Say something."

I could have said a number of things, though none mattered to him like they did to me. I might have reminded him that in my vivid imagination we had been thrust together to complete some cosmic riddle I wasn't convinced we'd yet solved. In some other life, I was sure our hearts had beat as one until ripped asunder, twin souls meant to meet again. These kinds of strong intuitions I'd had about us from the first. Or maybe I fabricated these flights of fancy to buffet the harsh reality of how crushing and cruel life can be about what is given and what is taken away. I thought our bond was karmic, destined. He thought our meeting was an accidental pleasure, perhaps more complicated than he bargained for, but just for fun.

I should have suggested to him how I believed we were meant to awaken each other physically, emotionally, mentally and spiritually. How he may have been meant to understand and love himself more fully through me, and together we were meant to experience an emotional integrity, a deeper intimacy, each through the other. I wish I had said those things because I believed them to be true, although we didn't achieve them. Here he was again, acting as though he'd been thrust toward me against his will. I could say I understood that, but I reveled in it. He didn't.

"Are you trying to torture me, Jackson? Are you enjoying yourself? I hate this. You've done this before, gone back and forth, undermining my confidence, playing on my insecurities. You know I've never understood why you pursued me in the first place. I mean, well, why you would want to be lovers with me, considering everything. I have no idea why we lasted this long either." I stammered, my self-esteem evaporating, my self-doubt one long run-on sentence. I did not want him to feel my weakness or see me cry.

"Damn it, why do you always say that shit? Yeah, the difference in our ages is a factor that's hard to ignore. But you know that fact isn't the main thing. I don't know what the hell the main thing is. It's weird. You come to me in the goddamn flesh and I can't resist. You know it. I can't escape you. What am I supposed to do with this? It doesn't fit anywhere."

He was right, of course. We didn't fit into our larger lives. He was living and thinking into his future, as he should have, I guess. As for me, I had the benefit of years, the luxury of a rear-view that revealed how precious is the time here and now. Tomorrow may arrive but doesn't make any promises.

The profound feelings of love and familiarity I experienced for him I now believe to be merely a hint of the ultimate longing that only a conscious reconnection with The Divine Beloved can satisfy. No human experience can fulfill that. Sometimes, though, when we sat in silence, our eyes the only intercourse or those times we made true love together, we came closer to The Bliss.

Now, he wanted to say goodbye again and though we weren't obliged, we stood at the edge of our personal sinkhole of nastiness as a way to divest ourselves of each other. Isn't that devolution common when you need to make a break, when you've tried before, but just can't? Against my deepest true feelings, I plunged into our stink-hole.

"Leave, Jackson. We've done all this before. I'm tired of your fucking vacillation. So go home, get on with your duties once and for all. I wish you luck, truly. You'll need it."

"Don't try to make me guilty for having a family. I was having a hard time with my wife back when we started, and I've explained all this to you before. I love her and we need to make it work, for our kids. He lowered his eyes and studied the floor. "I have my kids to think about. Family first."

"Right. Whatever. You shoved them all aside when you wanted to. You're so self-absorbed." A venomous spew was brewing within me I knew I should contain, would profoundly regret if I didn't, but it boiled over. "I've done everything I can to add to your life. You had the advantage of my hospitality, even as you allowed your family, especially your so-called wife, to suck everything but your dick dry, so fuck you. Oh wait, didn't I do that for you too? You want the story to end? It's over. There's the door." Brilliant. Why couldn't I just rein myself in?

"You and your damn temper, and that mouth. Feel better now? We go through this every time. You're mean. Where does this get us?"

"Why do we go through this? Where does it get us? It gets me nowhere. It gets you what you want until you change your mind again. You're mean and you're a fucking dumbass." Crap. I was acting like a middle schooler.

"Nice. Aren't you supposed to be this woman of wisdom? You're the one who makes up stories and fairytales and believes them. Check the clock, Savannah. Isn't it about time for you to grow up? You're always saying that to me. Shouldn't you wake up and act your age for once?"

"Low blow, Jackson." Damn his eyes, he was right even if he didn't understand the whole picture. I did wake up. I did embellish the story the way I wanted because it was *my* story. He had his own version. "I'm a free spirit, Jackson. I regret you can't appreciate that. Maybe you've never been free, but you're free to go. Do it, please. Now. End of story."

"Right. Okay, fine. We've been here before too. Let's try to be civil. We're still friends."

"Friends? We never had the same definition of what friendship entails. We're not friends, or are you talking again about friends with benefits? You want to be fuck buddies whenever you're not getting properly laid at home?" *Why can't I just shut up?*

"Low blow, Savannah. But why not? We're good that way. The best. Why can't we can keep that part going?"

Dumbass. I pointed to the door. "Leave." I whispered, eyes about to spill, my voice and heart cracking for the last time. Al least I hoped we wouldn't have to do all this again.

Now some years have passed and we still haven't disconnected from each other's lives or severed our energetic link. Neither of us seems capable of completely letting go. We stay in touch. I have simply had to acknowledge that we experienced an unexpected and unexplainable love for each other. I can accept that, but I could never be sure of what our attraction meant for him.

In spite of other delightful and sometimes, I must admit, better—well, at least more attentive—lovers I've experienced in the interim, he is still the one who comes into my dreams. He is still the one I choose to connect to physically and mentally by just a lovely memory.

We no longer make love or time for each other, but I can put aside what didn't work for us. I continue to nurture a physical yearning for him now and then for the sheer pleasure it brings me. My body rejuvenates. I dream of him, pull his energy to me and my cells begin to vibrate and regenerate. Often when I do, he'll call as if out of the blue. He'll say he suddenly thought of me and wanted to check in, but I know he felt my essence merge with his. I still sense when he is thinking of me in the same way at the same moment. He never understood the power of our energetic link. I may not understand either but I simply accept that we are linked in timeless relationship

He left such an impression of himself within me, that if I close my eyes and conjure him, I can viscerally taste his full luscious lips on mine. I surrender to the memory of his touch, the contrast of our skin, his scent, his hands exploring my body, the way we fit, having sex with him, making love with him.

Remembering how he moved inside of me recreates the exquisite sensations again and I am able to dissolve into orgasmic bliss. It's a residual blessing I can't explain. I loved waking up, with him.

What's Love Got to Do with It?
  ~ *Tina Turner*

This Does *NOT* Make Me A Cougar!

Theoretically, I suppose I started the flirtation, but truth be told, I had no expectations. I had enrolled in one of those free online dating sites with a silly name. Whenever I had the time and needed a bit of comic relief, I would log onto the pages of so-called computer-generated matches. Reading those profiles provided both a laugh and a lament on a lazy morning.

The men in my age bracket—which is, let's just say, older—claim to love holding hands, taking long walks on the beach or curling up by a romantic fire sipping wine on a rainy day. Their photo album features them with sporty baseball caps almost hiding their balding heads. Holding that just-caught giant slimy fish can't disguise their protruding bellies. The photos are generally taken somewhere in the wilderness because they claim to love camping or hiking. They might also be found kneeling close to some flowers in their yard indicating they know a thing or two about gardening. At least one picture will feature their dog. Often they'll choose a shot of themselves mid-swing, against a background of fairways, greens, or golf cart. Occasionally there's one taken from a distance, presumably them skiing down Mt. Everest, unrecognizable in gear, goggles and down. Each confesses to being a great guy and claims everyone believes they look and act 20 years younger than they are.

The men ten years younger are shown standing next to their Harley, mountain bike, hot rod, dog, or drinking buddies. They dig live music and provide lists of their favorite bands and clubs. They might be planning a hike across the crest of the Andes on their next vacation. If the lady prefers, kicking back with a margarita on a beach somewhere is fine too. Most confess to seeking a good-looking, easygoing, sexy woman who wants to keep things simple while sharing these activities as well as some "affection." This is emphasized since she needs to know this guy's still got what it takes.

The men 20 years younger love their kids every other weekend (and they're certain you will, too). They are into fitness and earning large sums of money someday. They claim they've moved on from their divorce, and are excited about getting back into the "game."

All of them attempt to flatter me by saying how young I appear and assuring me that age is not a factor. Age is a factor no matter what they may say. The brazen will even admit to being curious about what 'It' would be like with an older experienced woman.

The men who initiate contact with me seem certain I will be interested in them no matter how disparate the things we say in our profiles are. Most are impatient. They want my number, they want to connect so we can chat and arrange to have coffee, a glass of wine, lunch, or dinner, and they want get started right away. It's difficult to take any of them seriously.

On one particularly grey Sunday morning, an intriguing photo appeared on my page of prospects. He'd chosen a couple of excellent professional headshots in black and white. I opened his profile at once, delighted that anyone at all had captured my attention enough to investigate further. He's younger, of course.

I decided to write a quick note to explain that his appearance on my pages was a sweet surprise. On this lazy rainy morning, I was still laying around in my jammies, enjoying a second cup of coffee, and grateful for nothing more pressing to do than amuse myself by wasting time online.

I confessed to him I considered his appearance on my pages an omen to renew my enthusiasm for pleasant surprises. I added that it was too bad he was so young, or that I wasn't. He responded at once, playfully accusing me of trying to start something.

I wrote back:

"I had no intention of trying to start something, although I've coaxed an immediate response from you, so I guess something is starting. You must be aware those pro shots of you are attractive. You chose them. I initially responded to the appearance of your photos on my pages. Then when I read your profile, I got a kick out of how you present yourself. I'm assuming you have also read my profile now. I merely noted you are younger. This does not, however, make me a cougar. Enjoy your day."

He replied instantly:

"You're being evasive.

Why use the term cougar?

I like to think of any woman over 40 as my peer.

So what are you trying to start?"

To which I responded:

"I don't think I am being evasive.

I consider myself a peer of all.

Now something has started of its own accord.

I am still not *trying*.

As for the term cougar, I don't use it.

Not vivid enough for me."

Him:

"Not vivid enough?

Heh.

What term would you use?"

Me:

"Heh? Electronic transmissions in lieu of you know, conversation, can be subject to wildly diverse interpretations, and are likely to be misperceived by the recipient, in this case me.

What the heh?

I don't need a term.

But since you inquired, if I were to contemplate what 'cougar' means in this derogatory context, I'd be forced to confess I don't understand how a mountain lion applies to me, a woman of a certain age.

My personal application would be something closer to delightful possibility or even delicious opportunity."

Now him:

"Delightful possibility?

Delicious opportunity?

Now I think we're on the same wavelength. When might you be free for some, you know, conversation so we can eliminate any chance of being wildly, you know, misperceived?"

Now me again:

"Are you French? Were I not so self-assured I might, you know, think you're mocking me.

We can meet. I'll contact you."

Later we exchanged phone numbers and emails. Rex invited me to choose a quiet place with good red wine so we could meet and, well, I had to wonder what he had on his mind. I imagined we could enjoy some edgy conversation over dinner. We might like each other, but I didn't expect much more.

One thing I've learned over time is that too many expectations get in the way of noticing and enjoying what is happening right before me. He was pursuing me and I was flattered. I also felt as though at least I was drifting in the right direction. He was only 12 years younger instead of 23, as one of my last love affairs had been.

Here an emphatic clarification is in order. This last revelation definitely does not make me a cougar. Cougars are wild animals, hungry, stalking predators. I am neither stealthy nor starving. I am a healthy woman entertained by the prospect of delightful conversation and delicious sex with a handsome young man. Does this make me a cougar? I think not.

We met the next evening at my favorite local bistro. Rex was already seated in the reserved booth when I arrived.

"Savannah." He stood up and stepped out to greet me. We shared a warm inviting hug lasting just a little longer than is customary. He had the most alert mischievous brown eyes and he seemed to be taking me in, appraising me.

"Savannah," he said again under his breath, "A perfect name for you. You're even more stunning than your pictures."

I noted he did not add, for your age, and replied, "How charming. Thank you, Rex. You sound surprised."

He laughed. "Just a little. I've met several women who neither looked nor acted anything like their online profile. You fit the data: blonde hair and green eyes. I'll add gorgeous and confident to the stats as well. This is not always the case."

"That's a fact." I agreed. Extremely charming, I liked him already. Delightful possibility.

"Let's sit down," he suggested. We'd been standing close facing each other, holding hands, scarcely aware of our surroundings. A server lurked near, unsure of how to approach us. We held each other's gaze, slid into the booth, taking seats across from one another. I had the sudden impression that if we sat too close, we might forget about ordering, or talking, or even where we were altogether. He continued holding my hand from across the table and ordered a lovely translucent Pinot Noir. I slid my hand from his as we touched our glasses in the same lingering way we embraced. Delicious opportunity.

No, it's not always like this. I couldn't help myself. When I want to connect with someone, anyone, but in this case a striking man who had captured my full attention, I desire to create a comfortable environment so they become familiar and at ease with me. I'm rather skilled at this. Perhaps he noticed. He certainly responded as though he were comfortable. I don't always make the effort. It's not always like this.

"Enjoying yourself?" He asked. "I hope so because I am." He sipped his wine with the practice of a connoisseur. "How does this pinot suit you?"

It was perfect. The ambiance of the bistro, perfect. Mouth-watering aromas of lamb roasting over the open applewood fire from the cook station wafted through the bistro. Our server brought us a basket of warm, fresh-baked bread with herbed butter. He continued to smile into the moment. Perfect.

"Tell me why your work is like eating chocolate cake every day. Didn't you describe your job this way?" He laughed. His enthusiasm showed when he explained his work as creative director with a small firm developing a large project. While he spoke I took in every nuance of his tone, demeanor and presence. How his facial expressions hinted at his sense of humor, how his eyes stayed focused on me, how he reacted to my interest in what he said, how delightful and delicious I felt in his company. Perfect.

Our server returned with the list of specials and we decided to share the roast lamb, garnished with braised apples and savory herbed mashed potatoes. The prelude of a light citrus-dressed arugula salad topped with maple-glazed walnuts made the meal, again, perfect.

Yes, we enjoyed ourselves. We clicked. We resonated. We ate slowly, savoring every morsel of food, every sip of wine. The way he observed me with such focused attention told me he wanted to kiss me and I already knew I would encourage him to. This realization stirred my innate sensual curiosity and I tingled with anticipation when the message bolted south through my body and rang the buzzer between my legs.

He was quite handsome, that mouth, those silvery curls, dressed all in black. Wasn't his sweater cashmere? I sensed he also possessed a heady mix of intelligence and wit. Nothing is more intoxicating to me. I had no difficulty imagining his kiss would be a sumptuous dessert.

He must have noticed a change in my demeanor. My heightened desire and directed interest in his lips caught his attention and he sighed. "Shall we ask for the dessert menu, perhaps a cognac? A few more days to sit here and prolong this tantalizing moment?" He proved to be a delight beyond charm.

We finished dining, ordered a cognac and settled the check. I was enjoying everything about this encounter; the food, wine, cognac, the conversation, the sensuality, and now, I had to admit, the prospect of more. We couldn't tear ourselves away. We closed the place.

I must confess here: I have been scolded by friends and family for not being as cautious as I might or should be. I knew for certain he was not a rapist, a serial killer, or a terrorist. Of that I was confident. The bistro had closed and we were the only guests remaining. The staff glanced in our direction while performing their tasks, willing us to leave. Neither of us wanted to end the evening. With no option at that hour but to go to some bar, I invited him back to my place for tea.

On this wintry Monday evening I scanned my rearview mirrors as he followed me home. I hadn't thought beyond the moment and this unexpected turn of events overwhelmed me with anxiety. My full tummy fluttered with butterflies, and my confidence dissolved with the thought of him in my home. Still, something about him made me want to stretch out time.

When we had made the date yesterday, I hadn't expected more than a pleasant dinner. Now many delightful and delicious thoughts were crowding my better judgment. Though I'm prone to recklessness and recognized that tonight we were on the same wavelength, as we parked our cars and he followed me to the door, I decided we would not have sex.

The moment we stepped through the door he took me in his arms and kissed me tenderly on the forehead. We studied each other's eyes a moment before he kissed me on my lips. He held me closer. I kissed him in return and everything changed. We discovered we must kiss. We had to kiss, we needed to kiss.

I led him into the living room and curled up next to him on the couch. He brushed his hand over my breast as if by accident. I shuddered, my pert nipples reminding other parts of my body of their purpose. I kissed his neck and nibbled on his ear. He let out a long, deep sigh.

"Let's go to your room. Please." He took my hand and started to get up.

"I'm not going to have sex with you, at least not tonight." I whispered, all of a sudden shy.

"That's probably best," he replied unconvinced, kissing my throat and sliding his hands under the front and back of my soft loose sweater. With expertise, he unlatched my bra, gliding his hands over my back and ribs. I shivered as he cupped my breasts, calling my nipples to stand at attention. His tongue probed through my lips, discovering mine.

"I'll bet we could find a way to work around your decision if it's still your intention. Of course, I will abide by whatever you say." His gallant gesture impressed me. I believed he meant it, however practiced he might be. My proclivities toward, and lack of resolve in resisting, sensual pleasures relaxed. My concern at bringing him home was forgotten along with the teakettle.

The couch was comfortable and accommodated our passionate inquiries, but he said, "Let's go to your room. Although your couch is pleasant, I'm sure your bed is even more so. My back will be grateful,"

I should have probably insisted we stop then and say good night. I didn't nor did l want to. "I'm smack in the middle of my monthly," I confessed. "Tonight is not the most opportune timing."

Without a moment's hesitation he traced my lips with his finger and repeated, "I'll bet we could find a way to work around your decision, if you intend to hold to it. Of course, I will honor whatever you say. Vivid is not an exaggerated description of you, but I'll admit I'm surprised to find you so sweet, almost innocent."

He's delicious. "Almost innocent?" I giggled. "Come with me, then," I whispered as I kissed his ear.

"That's exactly what I want to do," he laughed. I led him into my room and lit several candles. "Perfect," he said and French-kissed my neck.

We stood holding hands, contemplating my bed. He smiled. Mischievous, I thought, although hesitant might better describe me at the moment. The flickering candlelight cast a welcome enticing hue over the room. I reached to open my bed to us, pulling the down comforter back. Still clothed, we curled into each other as comfortable and unselfconscious as if we'd been lovers forever.

He took my face in his hands and gazed into my eyes, so deep I wondered if he might penetrate my brain, my thoughts. With no effort he overcame my usual sassy veneer, his tender care for me as visceral as his desire. What a delicious surprise.

"I haven't experienced a close connection like this in years," he mumbled.

This rang true for me as well. I require a bond in order to make love. Sometimes I can manufacture the illusion of connection for myself and extend it to my partner so we can relax into our sexuality. But here in this moment with Rex, I didn't need to. We were both vulnerable.

How strange to consider less than 30 hours ago we were strangers, flirting and sparring on the internet. I reached for him and kissed his lips, my eager body quivering with the pleasure of touching him. We were meant to share this experience. Lying with him now was surely the right thing to do.

We made out. Is that still the term? Not tentatively either, I must confess. Piece by piece, various articles of clothing were peeled off and tossed aside. First to go were my sweater and bra then his yummy cashmere, t-shirt and socks.

Hands and lips invited themselves to touch and fondle wherever they desired. Every sensation took place in a dreamy fluid state of slow motion. Our skin began to have a strange magnetism, each to the other. We sank into each other's eyes for what seemed like eons. All our senses were focused on one another, and we became energetically fine-tuned.

His tongue went exploring as if on safari causing rivulets of shivering sensation on my nerves. Our hands and fingers acted as scouts seeking sensitive and erotic destinations. Our lips knew just where to make camp, stake claims, plant kisses, and deliver soft love bites. Entwined, he made me come with the slightest touch and gesture, an unexpected seismic shock undulating through us both. He took me over the edge and brought me back again. We made love as if nothing were more important and we had all the time in the world.

We didn't really have sex, well, not consummately. We did, however, find out a few important facts about each other. He discovered me to be ultra-sensitive to his every touch, responsive and multi-orgasmic. I discovered him to be sensual, tender and impressively hung with an admirable degree of self-restraint. We spent hours quietly talking, making out, making love. We were enraptured as though our coupling were the most natural thing to do, the only thing to do. But we didn't actually do it.

It was also impossible to stop. Each time either of us became cognizant of the hour, we would kiss each other, a last kiss, a goodbye kiss, and our passion would overcome us again. He had started an intense project at work and needed to facilitate an important meeting early in the morning. At last he forced himself to get up and dressed. We lingered at my back door, a last kiss heaven, far beyond the erotic preview that kindled such a fire.

After he drove away, I was wide awake with the pleasure of him, with the unexpected turn of events. I wanted him. Even if we never met again, if this were the only night we ever spent together, what a grand night!

The next morning he emailed me from work to tell me how he couldn't get a damn thing done. His mind kept wandering.

Mine too. Aftershocks. Something in this explosion of surprises inspired me to confess the effect he had on me.

I emailed him back and said:

"I've come to distract you further. Is your mind drifting, wandering to the way our lips couldn't stop kissing? The softness and pleasure? The tender exploration? The urgency and desire? Mine is.

Is your mind lost in remembered touches your body continually re-experiences viscerally? Mine is.

Has your mind developed a mind of its own, taking up residence in every secret naughty place in your body? Mine has.

What about tongues, eyelashes and earlobes?

Are you unable to explain why your mouth is etched in a permanent grin? Does anything at the moment seem more important? Don't answer that one please."

But he does answer:

"No, nothing seems more important right now. That's the problem. I need to work but my mind wanders back to last night. Those hours return to me in delicious detail.

I can't do anything but dwell in the tenderness, the exploration, the urgency, the desire. I still feel the pressure of your body on mine. I remember how you came again and again, your warmth when you curled into my arms afterwards. I'm perpetually aroused and pacing around my office getting nothing done.

I think about how we kissed, how the slightest gesture ignited us and I how last night with you made me come alive after so many years of darkness.

But, mostly I think about how it will be to go further with you, make love with you. It will probably be like the first few times I ever made love, when the raw power of it all was still like a mountain crashing down on me. So, no, nothing seems more important right now."

We made plans for him to return on the weekend, only a few eternal days away. We haven't even been completely naked together yet and intercourse is almost an incidental on its way to an absolute. We spent hours in deep physical inquiry of each other. We made love and experienced an immediate and vulnerable intimacy. Though we'd just met, this is what happens when lust takes over. All one can think about is consummation.

He called and said, "I've hidden my profile on the dating site until we sort out what is happening with us. I don't want to be distracted and I don't want to be bothered. I want to discover you in depth and detail."

"I'll do the same," I assured him. "I'm looking forward to Friday. The memory of your touch makes me shiver in anticipation."

"Till Friday, and touching you."

At the moment, neither of us is paying the slightest attention to the fact of the significant difference in our age. At the moment this is not an issue. At the moment age is not the point. The realization will steal into the garden like a slithering serpent sometime later. At the moment our imaginations are occupied with the prospect of touching, kissing, making love, having sex. He is pursuing this avidly as am I, but I can assure you: this does *not* make me a cougar.

Lovers know what they want, not what they need.
  ~ Pubilius Syrus (1st Century B.C.)

Playing Doctor

I spotted him first. We've never met in person, but as I inch my way through the crowd toward the gate, I recognize Doctor Robert instantly from the photos he's sent me. Even from a distance I sense his tension as he scans the passengers disembarking their flights, pressing into the terminal. When his eyes land on me, he waves. His smile is broad. My own trepidation is eased somewhat.

"Thank God." He takes my bag and clasps my hand. I look up at him puzzled. He clarifies with a wink, "Well, pictures can be deceiving, wouldn't you agree, Savannah?" Anchoring his free hand to the small of my back, he guides me through the scrambling swarms of travelers. "Thank God yours are a true likeness of you, though you're, shall I say, more diminutive than I might have thought, and your eyes more green than your photos reveal, you have the same enchanting smile and healthy teeth. I am not disappointed."

Healthy teeth? "So I passed inspection, cleared security?" My laugh is on the edge of uneasy. Not disappointed? Am I? He's much taller and his presence more formidable than I anticipated. The lines etched around his lively brown eyes a little deeper than his pictures show. His early retirement in the dry Sedona sun makes his age more apparent. Still, he's fit and energetic and I'm looking forward to the next couple of days in the high desert.

"You'll do nicely," he grins and winks again. "I've a lovely weekend planned, and now that we've managed to make our way out of this circus we can get started. Here's my car."

He's edgy. It's an essential element of his character, maybe even part of his allure. Even though I'm prone to navigating the edge, I'd never have agreed to visit him sight unseen, but the last several months of emails and phone conversations gave us a fair assessment of each other. His self-confidence is excessive to the point of comic arrogance. I've been accused of the same at times, my bravado more a learned compensation for underlying feelings of vulnerability. Still, we've laughed about how our teasing, sarcastic banter can descend into calling each other out with a rapid descent into foul language. This he enjoys, and rare is my opportunity to interact with someone who can or will take it and fling it back. I get a kick out of him.

Doctor Robert cruises internet dating sites claiming to be looking for a partner. This may be true, but he is also trolling for sex. He's not alone in his endeavors. Anyone dipping a toe into the hopeful hunter's world of virtual love is aware of an underlying current of sexual exploration, whatever the pretense. No misunderstanding where our interest in each other is leading; we've talked about everything happening in our current and past lives, including sex, in depth and detail. Once we decided to meet in person, I felt comfortable enough to accept an invitation to his home for a couple of days. He sent pictures of his stunning house in the high sunny desert and offered me a private room and bath. I decided to take a chance. Not a difficult decision. I've never been to Sedona and late fall in Seattle is already as bitter cold and sodden as winter.

"I think you'll love this compilation of some of my favorite songs." He expertly negotiates the midday city traffic, honking his horn and waving off anyone impeding his way. Once on the freeway though, we both fall into an uncharacteristic silence. I am now self-conscious, even a little shy. The drive out from

Phoenix to Sedona is almost two hours. In the quiet, listening to 'his' songs, I begin to tense again, on alert, as if in the absence of our customary chatter, we're energetically sizing one another up. "Listen to this exquisite rendition of "Over the Rainbow" by the late Eva Cassidy," he says, his eyes misting with unexpected emotion. "She will bring you to tears." I know the song, of course. I've even heard this version and it *is* beautiful, but tears? What do I think of this guy?

"Is it the lyrics of this song or the tragic death of a gifted singer that moves you so?"

"Both. Life is tragic. Love is tragic. But I've designed this pleasant weekend to distract us from the shortcomings of eternal tragedy."

"Eternal tragedy . . . hmmmm." The song ends and his demeanor changes, becoming animated and enthusiastic as he details his plans for our activities over the weekend.

"We'll begin by settling in and freshening up before our dinner reservation at L'Auberge, my favorite French bistro in town. Tomorrow we'll hike. I've selected a mildly challenging trail where you can enjoy a view of the valley and monuments from a different angle. I hope you possess the stamina to keep up." His sarcastic taunt marks a return to his more usual behavior and even though the underlying curiosity and tension between us is tangible, I'm somehow more at ease.

"I can keep it up, I only hope you can." His attention had been on the road but now his glance assesses me from the inside out. As he nods and faces forward the amused grin that spreads across his face puts me back on edge. I struggle with a tangle of impressions and feelings. Unable to settle or comfort myself, I'm equal parts amusement, anticipation, and nervous energy.

As we arrive at his place in the valley outside town I'm clear why this Jewish doctor from the Bronx, New York, transplanted himself. His airy home is nestled into a secluded hillside and opens onto an unobstructed panoramic view of the famous Red

Rock Cathedral formations. I leave my bag in the foyer and he directs me to the two rooms on the first floor from which I may choose. They're both modest in relation to the rest of the house, uninvitingly furnished with a single bed, a side table and cluttered with Giants football memorabilia—Big Blue, as he calls his NY home team with enthusiastic affection.

Upstairs, the main floor is also sparse and feels almost uninhabited. Alphabetized bottles of vitamins in a neat row line his kitchen counter. The surprising lack of art and color on the bare walls, the absence of plants which would thrive in this light airy environment, and no personal belongings anywhere, make this beautiful space seem un-lived in. He'd told me, in one of our phone conversations, he'd moved out here seven years ago. But does he *live* here? There's no sense of comfort or ease about this beautiful place or him.

Even though every window offers spectacular views, he chose a tiny closet on the landing just outside the kitchen to house his office. Strange. His computer is on. Pencils and sticky notes are placed in symmetrical alignment. This tiny space is where he spends much of his time. The entire scene is odd and I'm forced to realize he is quite a bit more odd than I first imagined.

With an expansive smile, he casually drapes himself into his office chair, more at ease now in this cramped windowless sanctuary. I tease him about his internet trolling enclave. He chuckles and explains today he is following bidding on some items listed with eBay.

As he turns his attention to the screen, an unusual malaise settles over me. I hope coming down here was the right decision. I remember a particular phone conversation when Doctor Robert assured me with passionate conviction—should I decide to spend a weekend with him—that he would make me the recipient of his legendary expertise. His lips, tongue and hands would guarantee sexual pleasures I had never experienced before. I laughed and teased him about making claims he couldn't back with action. Here now, I am decidedly ill at ease.

As I glance down the hall into the master bedroom—his room—a few feet away, I stroll over to the open doorway and look inside, wondering what to expect next. At the threshold to where intimacy between us is likely to happen, if indeed any does, I try to assess the situation I find myself in. I'm not uncomfortable with him particularly. I'm uncomfortable in general.

I must be more fatigued than I realize because I don't hear or even sense him move until he's standing close behind me kissing me softly on the back of my neck. I flinch, the surprise of his touch jolting my nerves even though his kiss is rather pleasant and welcoming. It's more sensual than I'd anticipated.

"I want you to stay in here with me tonight, Savannah," he said. "Should you find yourself uncomfortable, you can always retire downstairs. I promised you when we decided to meet, I'll respect whatever you want." Though he's edgy, thus far, he is also a gentleman, even affectionate and attentive. Maybe he's as nervous as I am. If so, he hides it well. "Allow me to draw you a bath so you can freshen up and relax." He leads me through his room into the master bath. With a dramatic flourish, he reveals an alcove with a welcoming sunken tub. The surrounding full-length windows open to a secluded cactus garden outside walled in by the red rock hillside. "I seldom use this room. I prefer showers, which I take downstairs. Consider this yours for your stay."

I accept with gratitude. Our dinner reservation isn't for several hours and I am suddenly overwhelmed and exhausted from the flight, the drive, and my nerves. He adds scented salts to the filling tub and leaves me. In anticipation and relief I sink into the hot lavender-scented, magazine-perfect bath. I'm alone and serene until an amusing thought flits across my mind: this is, well, just what the doctor ordered.

I inhale the fragrance and begin to relax. Gazing at the beauty outside these windows, my breath catches when I see him watching me in the full-length mirror that reflects into his room. He winks and strips down to his shorts and tank top before returning to his computer closet sanctuary. My serenity jarred, I wait. Silence. When I realize I'll be granted my privacy I begin to unwind, sighing in relief, conscious of the decision to ignore my body's first alert signal.

The hot fragrant water coaxes my tense muscles to soften and the lavender scent soothes my frayed nerves. The play of sun and shadows dancing across the jagged stone formations outside is dreamlike, as if I am bathing out in the rock and cactus garden. I drift in luxurious tranquility. Time slows, my eyes close and I drift. Without warning, Doctor Robert is standing at the edge of the tub observing me with intense curiosity.

"Oh!" I'm dismayed to discover the towel is out of my reach. I wait, anxious to discover what he is going to do. He's rooted where he stands, and though his expression is bemused, he is at the same time absorbed in keen scrutiny of my body. I reflexively try to cover up with my arms and hands.

"You surprised me, Robert. Hand me a towel, please?"

He laughs, "Am I your slave already?" He offers me the towel but as I reach he lifts it out of my grasp and laughs again.

"The towel, please?" My instincts warn me; if this is a game, it's on.

"Stand up, Savannah. Let's take a good look at you first." He reaches for my hand to assist me with a firm grasp and I reluctantly step out of the tub. He drapes me in a fluffy blue towel, gently patting me dry. He folds the towel just so before hanging it evenly on the rack. I stand naked before him, nervous and nauseated, while he fills his palms with almond oil. With slow, gentle strokes, he methodically polishes me. I stand statue still, self-conscious and trembling. All of this seems a bit too soon. He says nothing, relishing his sensuous exploration. My apprehension dissolves into pleasure as his fingers mesmerize every tingling inch of me.

"Come with me," he whispers, kissing the back of my neck again as he pulls me into the bedroom and onto his bed. My nakedness and vulnerability distress me yet I willingly allow his soothing hands to continue their exploration. His soft kisses relish my throat, my lips, my wrists. An unexpected tenderness in his eyes disarms me as I ease into the comfort and the pleasure of his touch. His lips press intensely against mine, eliciting a rush of confusing sensations. His hands cup my breasts, his tongue exploring, probing, blazing a trail across my chest and down my belly. Every place his mouth touches me sizzles and comes alive. I reach for him, with my body responding, desiring more. He halts then, props himself up on his elbow and gazes at me.

"Is this a preview of coming attractions, Robert?" I hear my voice belie my feelings of vulnerability and exposure, of desire interrupted.

"I promised you pleasures and I believe that is why you are here, is it not? Or were you merely curious about the scenery?" I reach for a throw draped over the edge of the bed. "Are you chilled, Savannah?"

"No, I just. . ." He licks the inside curve of my elbow. "Robert, listen I. . ." He nuzzles the dent above my clavicle.

"Savannah, I find you, in the flesh, far more tantalizing than I had anticipated. Far more receptive, and I must say, delightfully more vulnerable than I expected. I am very much looking forward to exposing you to unprecedented pleasures that I am confident you will not merely enjoy, but deeply desire and ultimately crave. Now, where shall I begin?"

"Robert, wait, I—" He nibbles his way up my neck while his fingers massage my breasts and somehow at the same time wander between my thighs. He rolls my nipples between his finger and thumb while investigating the shape and texture of my clitoris, burrowing into my vagina and eliciting tremors of pleasure. Within minutes I am about to come.

He senses this. "Hold that sensation. my lovely," he instructs me, slowing down his caresses and kissing my belly. Again I'm interrupted. I close my eyes and slow my breath, attempting to follow Doctor Robert's instruction. I reach to slip off his shorts, but he says, "Not yet." His fingers slip deeper into my vagina, honing in on my spot.

"Why not?" I gasp, reaching for him again.

"You're being a naughty girl, Savannah. I'm going to torture you with pleasure just as I promised." He chuckles and—like magic—fondles every last erotically charged cell of my anatomy at once.

"I'm going to come," I whisper in ecstasy.

"Suspend it," he commands, exhaling deeply, withdrawing. His flushed face and glazed eyes peer at me.

"I can't."

"Yes, you can."

"But why would I want to?" I plead, pulling back from the edge yet again. I want to touch his cock. He won't let me. I reach for him again and he pulls away, teasing me. "Robert, why not? I want to touch you too. Please."

"Not now, lovely. If you'll just relax and allow me to perform this procedure, you won't regret it and you will never forget it."

"A procedure?" What the hell does that mean? "What are you planning to do with me, Doctor?" I struggle to regain my composure. His teasing is making me uneasy again even as his hands and fingers return to manipulating the moist and pulsating cleft between my legs. I'm torn between demanding he stop and begging for more.

"All this is mere prep, my lovely," he whispers in my ear, then lowers his head to my mound. He sniffs as his mouth appraises my inner thighs. He wiggles his sizable snout into my vagina and shouts, "Fuck! You smell delicious. I'll sip that nectar right now."

He hoists my hips, spreads open my thighs and devours me, licking like a lollipop, triggering an explosion of orgasmic contractions, sending me into another world. His mouth a suction cup, his tongue swirls around my clit and my labia, dipping into my pulsing vagina. Intense waves of pleasure stun me. I'm speechless because not only am I passively allowing this man to gorge on me, I desperately want him to. I'm soon lost in writhing moaning sensations of unceasing intensity.

My climax builds toward an explosion yet I have no release. My body throbs, this pre-orgasm an unrelenting ecstasy. I lose my bearings, and all sense of my place in space. An atomic pulse radiates from my core, expanding in rippled shimmering waves toward infinity while in the same moment imploding to my depths. Vibrant, pulsating streams of pure joy gush from my essence. I've de-materialized. Clearly, I've ascended into heaven. I can scarcely discern the blurred in bliss edges of myself.

When at last I open my eyes, disoriented and confused, my body is still thrumming. Doctor Robert's mouth is a twisted grin. "I'm pleased to report that the procedure was a complete success, Savannah," he declares triumphantly.

Only when I hear him speak my name, do I begin to gather back in. I clutch him and murmur, "Oh God! Oh my God."

"Godly perhaps, but not God. I am a skilled doctor. A specialist, as I've previously mentioned. I suspected you had this level of explosive passion within you if only you would surrender to my provocations. We're off to an auspicious beginning, my dear."

Whatever on earth is he talking about? We are still on earth, aren't we? Never have I experienced a climax of such length or magnitude and my shimmering mind and body are disconnected.

We lay together in a timeless void. In some recess of my mind I'm aware that the afternoon light has faded to dusk. This is as close to orienting myself in time and space as I can come. All I know for certain is I can and have come. Magnificently. I hear my hoarse whisper, "Doctor Robert. What did you do to me?"

He props me up with a stack of pillows crowing, "Cock-a-doodle-dooooooo!" His response is so absurd, I'm compelled to laugh, the laughter bringing me back into my body. "Time to get up now, my lovely. We need to dress for dinner. You won't be disappointed there either."

I'm as uncoordinated as though drunk, sitting on the edge of the bed. I can't manage my limbs or think what to wear, but he hands me the long black linen skirt I arrived in only a few hours or eons ago. I'm grateful as he dresses me, buttons my blouse, and straps on my sandals. It's not until we're in the car, halfway into town, that I discover he neglected my panties and bra and I hadn't even noticed.

"Robert! I have no underwear." Oh my God!

"Yes, indeed," the doctor replies, with a sly grin. "All the better and easier, I might add, to explore you under the bistro table." Did I hear right? "Imagine this, if you will, Savannah. We're engaged in light conversation, enjoying our dinner, savoring a fine wine. You're clueless as to when I might desire you again, when I might use my stealth skills to entice you. Don't bother trying to stay alert to this, my lovely. As I've explained, I have plans for you and since intimately experiencing your vulnerabilities, not only have I learned what you want but I now know what you cannot resist."

"Wait!" What is he talking about? Seducing me in public, without my consent? I'm incensed. "Robert, you've overstepped, and clearly overestimated my uninhibited nature. But you greatly underestimate my resolve." How can I reassert myself to gain some control over this situation? More importantly, I now realize, how will I gain control over myself?

"No lame protests, if you please."

Doctor Robert is quite proud of being a New York-style smart-ass, encouraging the recalcitrant though not too repressed sass within me to spar with him. This was actually part of our attraction and initial turn-on. I can tell him to fuck off with impunity.

"Hold on, Doctor. Okay, yes, I more than enjoyed this afternoon's delight. And true, I might be looking forward to more. I'm not thrilled to admit I may not be able to resist, especially now you've proven to be the professional you claim to be. But believe me, no fucking way will I tolerate you usurping my free will with a public display of your skills. I hope you are just teasing me. Don't even think about embarrassing me."

He chuckles, his eyes never leaving the road. His right hand slides up under my skirt and his finger slips into my vagina before I register he's moved. I clench my thighs together.

"Damn you!" I snarl. He laughs and starts to crow again.

"I'm your slave; I'll do you in whatever way you want."

"My slave? More like I'm your slave. You don't do as I say at all."

"I never said I would do as you *say*, my lovely darling. I will, however, do what you want. It's your issue if you're confused about the difference between the two."

My thighs unwillingly loosen their grip as his magic fingers seek and find new range to roam. I try to make an important point here but can no longer remember what that is. He crows again and yanks his wet fingers out, leaving me midway to coming. Before taking the wheel with both hands, he caresses my cheek. In a flash his hand slips inside my shirt and pinches my nipple hard. That hurt! He crows again howling with delight. He's a relentless tease. I slug him in the shoulder.

"No need for violence now. You can pretend to be put out, but we both know you love the way your body responds. I understand how intolerable it must be for you to think you're at my mercy. In truth, you are only under my spell because you want to be. You might be resistant to the idea of surrendering to me, to the pleasure I so obviously bring you, but you are not powerless. In fact, my dear Savannah, I see you've no idea what kind of power you generate with your sexuality and the effect it is having on both of us. I hope this clears it up for you. In the meantime, a lovely dinner and the rest of the weekend lie before us."

His charming discourse and authoritative delivery make this assertion sound somehow plausible, but what powerful effect is he talking about? He's holding himself separate from me even as he bestows me with sensual pleasures I can't resist and don't want to resist. My mind is muddled. He's right. I'm confused, about everything.

We park in front of a vine-covered, buttery stucco bistro. "Here we are. This is my favorite place to dine. You will absolutely love the atmosphere and the food."

"I already love the romantic ambiance. How quaint and French. This is the most Toulouse-Lautrec-looking, Mediterranean bistro I can imagine in a place that looks nothing at all like France." The lovely distraction eases and relieves my confusing emotions about Doctor Robert.

"How astute, my lovely Savannah."

Seated across from one another at a small, secluded table, he orders a bottle of white Bordeaux without consulting the list. "I suggest the divine Pasta Primavera, my favorite." I glance over the menu and ask him about some of the other offerings only to discover he never bothered to sample anything else. When I ask him why not, he explains, "Why would I vary from what I know to be excellent?"

I wonder why he wouldn't give excellence a chance to go wide, but decide not to press him. I'm too deliciously mellow to kick in with the sarcasm I might enjoy at another time. Anyway, I fear he'll lap it up and I realize now that I have no idea what he might do in public.

Our waiter is a charming young man with a thick Spanish accent, trying in vain to sound French. He describes the Tarte Nicoise special with such a sensual flair that I order it. But when I glance across the table, I discover Doctor Robert scowling at me.

"What?" He's upset.

"I suggest the finest thing on the menu and you don't trust me enough to try it. You obviously value that fawning young flirt's suggestions over mine."

"Are you utterly mental? How can you possibly be upset about that? You've never even tried anything else on the menu to know if your choice is best. Why would you take it personally if I prefer something different?"

I prepared for an animated debate, the kind we fell into with ease over the phone before meeting in person, hoping he'd minimally control his volume. But to my surprise, he whispers, "cock-a-doodle-doo," wiggles his big toe between my legs and into my vagina so quickly, I nearly spill my wine in shock.

"What the hell? Did I give you permission to do that? Did I not make myself perfectly clear?" I gasp glancing around the bistro. Are we being observed? Fucking bastard.

"I believe we covered this already." he hisses, his impatience apparent. "I do not respond to what you *say* you want. I am responding to what you innately want, what your body craves. I realize this is not yet clear to you." Damn, he's right. The reality of his big toe teasing my clit under the table is precisely what I want, regardless of my protest. We lock eyes and I sip my wine, observing my body experience this odd unexpected sensation. "Do you grasp the situation now, my lovely?" He smirks, a cunning smile lurking in the crinkle of his eyes. His tongue laps the corner of his mouth as his toe slips over the lid of my clit and back into his sandal.

"Motherfucker." This is our first evening together and already my continuous experience of erotic pleasure should be sated, but instead I'm ravenous for more. I don't want to admit this to myself. I especially do not care to admit it to him.

When I decided to visit Doctor Robert, I understood that once we met in person, we would have sex if we found each other pleasing. We had agreed that if that were not the case, we would still enjoy the weekend together. And if we weren't able to get along, I would book a room in town with no hard feelings. Although he is quirky and I am not able to anticipate or predict his behavior as I am accustomed with most men, he doesn't frighten me. He's definitely discovered unexpected ways to pleasure me. Thus far his quirkiness is more disarming than pleasing but his nature is essentially kind. I like him.

Our dinners are elegantly presented. Mine is delicious; the wine is delightful. Relaxed, we dine leisurely. We chat amiably and casually, our pronounced sexual energy the punctuation. Our handsome young server returns, suggesting the specialty dessert, a rich torte with brandy-soaked cherries and thick sweetened cream. I'm easily persuaded.

"What do you think, shall we share one, Doctor?"

Robert shrugs noncommittally, "If it pleases you, my lovely."

The luscious confection arrives with our espressos, It's delicious. Robert takes one reluctant bite, smiles unconvincingly and declines another. When I ask why, he explains flatly that regarding desserts, he favors apple pie after chicken soup for lunch on Wednesdays. My laughter fades when I realize he's dead serious. Such a strange man.

As we drive back out to his house in the dark, he starts the same CD and track as on the drive from the airport. "You love this song, don't you?"

"Yes, this is a beautiful song and it's always first." He explains how he likes to start the music in order. I can't help wondering how deeply his need for routine and control goes.

We park, strolling up to the house, arms around each other's waists. He suggests we sit out on his front deck. "It's such a warm evening, even for Sedona. and the view, as you can clearly see, is wonderful. Sit here next to me, Savannah dear."

I want nothing more than to curl up in the cushioned double-seated swing and enjoy this spectacular scene before me. The moon is full and high above the giant red rock formations, casting a mysterious glow over the still landscape. We sit together like lovers, sweethearts holding hands. There's an almost ethereal feeling about the quiet darkness.

I turn to ask him about Sedona's famous magnetic attraction and discover that Doctor Robert is staring at me, with his deep brown eyes fairly glowing. I kiss him on the cheek, distracted by his intensity. "Thank you for a wonderful afternoon and dinner. You're a most gracious host."

"You're welcome, my lovely. You have made it my pleasure." He pulls me close, kissing me deeply and passionately. Turning me toward him, his hands resting lightly on my shoulders, he begins, "Listen, Savannah, I've given this some thought. We seem to be compatible on many important levels. You're one of the few women I've met who can handle me. You aren't reticent in the least to assert yourself with me. I admire that. You're quick-witted, a fine specimen of a smart-ass and as sexy as they come. I want you to think about looking at this weekend as a prelude to more weekends in the near future and perhaps even a more permanent alignment."

"A more permanent alignment?" I repeat, wondering if I heard him correctly. "What does that mean?" True, we've discovered that we have a strong physically energetic attraction. True, also, that we share a certain sense of humor and easiness with each other even when we do descend into heated sarcastic diatribes. But talking about a more permanent alignment, as in a committed relationship? This I cannot imagine. Not yet. How can he suggest as much so early in our story?

I speculate for a few moments how a scenario of *us* would look. He has declared he will never again live in a northern climate, in fact cannot begin to entertain the idea of leaving this valley. The Pacific Northwest has everything I love the most: mountains, trees, inland seas, ocean coastline, even prairie and rain forests. It's a microcosm of the USA. I can't imagine living here full-time, even as unique and beautiful as Sedona is. Plus, my home is filled with color and art, music and comfort. It's welcoming to family and friends. Doctor Robert would be miserable there. He has no family near and prefers it that way. He told me once that he requires and protects his privacy and rarely invites anyone to his home. I wonder about his friends and I wonder why I have become an exception.

"Well?" He peers deeply into my eyes waiting for a response.

"Well, don't you think it's slightly premature to consider a life change so monumental, Doctor? How can you be so sure already? We haven't even spent 24 hours together." His expression becomes unreadable, he continues to smile but his eyes betray no emotion. I am here for an erotic weekend. The concept of something more meaningful at this juncture is preposterous.

"You're right, of course, Savannah," he concedes, his tone measured. I wonder if he is somehow disappointed. "I'm confident you will have a change of heart when you experience the beauty and mystery of Sedona. Many more pleasures await you here. Now, let's go to bed, my lovely. We'll get some rest. I have a pleasant but challenging hike planned for us in the morning."

It's only 9:00 p.m. coastal time, my time. I'm not at all sleepy. "Let's sit a while longer. That moon over the Cathedrals is so beautiful, so etheric, I feel like we're on another planet."

"Is that honestly what you want?"

"Yes, it is what I want. Aren't you enjoying this romantic moonlight?

"It's lovely, yes." He presses close to me, his lips exploring that place on the curve of my neck triggering shivers while his hands expertly slip under my shirt and skirt. How does he know to touch me so intimately in just the right way? I become dizzy and disoriented again. It's immediate. A thought crosses my mind: Is he a spell weaver? I ask him if this is so.

"Whatever you wish to call it, Savannah."

I may not know him well, yet I can instantly become completely receptive to the intimacy that his tongue, lips and hands elicit. I have never experienced anything quite like this immediate and intense arousal with just a touch. I can't explain why I am so ultra-sensitive and responsive to him. Though we haven't actually made love together, I can scarcely imagine anything surpassing this afternoon's delight and suggest as much to him.

"Imagination should be boundless, my dear," he whispers. "Now please, let's go to bed. I want to make love to you the way you want it. I know what you want."

His lips and fingers are persuasive. Standing, he takes my hand, pulling me up and out of the swing and leads me into his room, the moon and rocks forgotten.

As I bend over my bag, digging for the gown I plan to wear, he comes behind me, unzipping my skirt and letting it drop to my ankles. He then unbuttons my shirt and pulls it from my body. Naked once again, I stand, sensing in him a new nervous tension. From behind, he molds my hips with his soft warm hands, sliding his fingers around to the front creases of my yoni, massaging his way to the center of my sensuality. Sighing deeply, softening to his touch, I turn to embrace him. We kiss, his emotion and passion enveloping me. I slide my hands over his torso and down his back, but he steps back slightly. He doesn't touch me now, incongruent with his demeanor a moment earlier. He seems hesitant, not at all exhibiting his usual assertiveness. Closing the gap between us, I slip my fingers into the waistband of his boxers. He tenses apprehensively and stands ramrod straight as I pull them to his knees.

What I see catches me off guard. He's not only limp, he has the tiniest pencil-thin dick I have ever seen on a grown man. I'm in shock, unable to take my eyes from it. I've seen fingers larger. Apparently he anticipated my reaction, for he launches into a practiced-sounding, "size is not important" lecture, stressing that technique—specifically his skill and expertise—is more valuable to me than a big cock. I'm mute. How can I tell him that a man-size penis matters quite a lot to me?

I begin to understand him from a different perspective now. He's learned to compensate skillfully for his physical lack just as a person with another kind of handicap does, like someone who is blind or deaf might develop another sense. He has fine-tuned the sensitivity of his lips, tongue and hands to such a degree, that women will overlook or perhaps simply stop caring that his cock could get lost in a keyhole.

He finishes his dissertation and we stand there, facing each other in silence. I don't know what to say. I have no idea what to do next. His sex organ, the body part of a man so necessary to me for the ultimate satisfaction of lovemaking, the part I not only appreciate but crave inside of me, is altogether unappealing. Worse, I have inadvertently hurt his feelings. What should I do? I haven't had an opportunity to discover what might please him yet and I wonder if I can override my current aversion to his lack of virility. I've never even been naked with a man who wasn't rock hard by this juncture.

Though his teeny flaccid cock will scarcely fill my mouth, still I decide to perform the magic that most men find irresistible. He reluctantly allows me to lay him back on the bed and take his puny penis into my mouth. He's tense, acting as if he's enjoying it, but he's acting. I know that. No matter what I do, and I am not without skills in this area, he never gets hard or anywhere close to coming.

"I'm saving it for the right time." he informs me, pulling away, as if this is an obvious explanation. "I prefer not to come too often."

I peer deeply into his eyes trying to get a sense of him, but he turns away from me. I hug him with as much tenderness as he will allow, hoping that he can feel my sincere affection for him more than my obvious disappointment in his equipment. I notice that he's placed the vial of almond oil on the side table. Pouring a little into my hands, I caress his perpetually tense body with long relaxing stokes. His tension eases somewhat but when I try to pleasure his miniscule shaft and little pong-pong balls, he tenses again, lying perfectly still, limp as a noodle, holding his breath.

He allows himself to receive my attention for only a few brief moments, before rolling aside. He then reaches for the bottle and pours some oil in his hands. He is taking charge again, touching me, stroking me in already tender swelling places. My mind is stuck, working over whether this mutual masturbation will be as close as we will come to making love together. He quickly distracts me from my lament. His sensitive hands, deft and practiced, seem to be cloning themselves, diverting my attention from any other expectations I might still be harboring.

"Stop thinking so deeply, Savannah. Why not simply lay back and enjoy the ride? You'll come to understand me better as time passes."

"I don't understand you at all, Robert. My confidence is undermined by not being able to arouse you."

"I'm sure that's a new experience for you, isn't it? Not to worry. You'll discover what arouses me besides arousing you. Relax. I'm enjoying this very much. Why don't you allow yourself to as well?"

"But, I want to be able to..." His touch is charged with astonishing voltage. I shiver into a juicy orgasm without him even approaching my innermost zones. His mouth dines on my labia, his tongue circling my clit and perineum. His fingers root deep into my vagina, tapping a secret message onto my spot. "Robert, I just want. . ." I can't hold a thought. I come again, more intensely.

Somehow he's kissing my neck and breasts and licking my clit all at the same time. Sensations compete for attention, every inch of my body beckoning him. He touches me just right in every way. I never have to wish for anything. I never have to ask him for anything. There are never any adjustments to be made. I come again and then again, now with trembling that overtakes my entire body and still he continues. I hear myself yelp like a coyote pup and this prompts him to come up for air and crow like a rooster.

"Cock-a-doodle-dooooooo!" he howls. We dissolve into peals of laughter, but he's not sidetracked for long, nor does he seem to tire of his craft. I'm undone but I'm not tired either. I do feel vulnerable and a bit helpless at how weird this intimacy feels. He would be moving inside of me by now if he were anyone else.

I would be begging for that if he were anyone else. His finger, wet with me, slowly and ever so gently circles my anus penetrating slightly. Now I tense for a moment. This is not something that I usually enjoy and I suddenly realize why. No one has ever touched me there in this inquisitive and intuitively sensitive way before.

One of his fingers is gently cruising around my anus, a thumb or something explores the back wall of my vagina, another finger presses my spot and another, or his tongue—I can no longer differentiate—is massaging my clit. My body undulates with pleasure, as he presses me against the bed.

I hear, then feel, a little vibrator on my nipples, before he masterfully applies it to every pulsating, dripping, swelling, ripe spot between my legs. I cry out now, my climax a tempest, a gale force raging. He eases and adjusts with my rhythms, but he doesn't stop. I think I beg him to but at last I begin to comprehend the dichotomy between what I might be saying and what I definitely want. Oh! I want it. I can protest and beg and say I can't take any more, but I want it. Nothing else matters more to me at the moment than this craving of his sexual heroin. I blow apart as though a wild desert wind were tossing and scattering me. At last it passes and my scattered pieces float to earth in stillness.

"Hold me." Am I crying? Tears are leaking from my eyes and running down my cheeks. I may have dissipated, dispersed to nothingness. "Hold me, Robert. Please hold onto me." I'm not sure if I am actually hearing my pleas out loud. Maybe I've come apart and am disappearing. Maybe I'm not even embodied anymore.

"I have you. Never worry about that my lovely darling. I'll hold you. I can hold you forever. Let yourself rest in that awareness. You are right here, here in Sedona with me."

At some point I become aware that indeed, I am enfolded into the long length of his body. He's holding me steady. His soft soothing kisses on the back of my neck and shoulder fix me to this point in time and space. He gently strokes me, and eventually I find myself again. I feel wonderful and at the same time so vulnerable it's almost frightening. Who is this man who has introduced me to my body in such a new erotic sensual way? We lay curled together and drift to sleep. Somewhere in the night he pulls the quilt over us and in the morning we haven't moved from that embrace. In this strange unexpected intimacy, we lay entwined like lovers. Nothing is amiss except the fact that we are not actually in love.

But we can sleep together. Who would have guessed that? Two tempestuous types like us, sleeping peacefully together through the night? This is an important test of compatibility for me. We slept comfortably together. I guess that's some measurement of a fit although not in accordance with my usual standards. He hasn't had to dip inside for me to speculate on the obvious in that area.

But when he awakens in the morning, he's hard, sort of. Though this phenomenon doesn't add much length or girth to his unit he still wants to use it. I want him to be able to if for no other reason than the sake of balance. "What about condoms?" I ask sleepily.

"We don't need one; I'm not going to come inside of you." And he means it. He doesn't. I scarcely notice him in there and he goes limp within minutes. I'm once again at a loss as to what to say or do. He has given me such incredible pleasure. I want to reciprocate, but how?

Finally I just ask, "How can I please you? What would give you the most pleasure? I guess I just don't do it for you." As I express this thought out loud, I feel suddenly sad. We're having a sex romp weekend, of which I am the sole beneficiary. I should be thrilled. I've been taken to heaven, and he is the vehicle. But he drops me off at the gates alone, unable—or is it unwilling?—to accompany me.

"It's not that I'm not into you, Savannah. I've tried to convey this to you over and over. You turn me on incredibly and I crave being able to do what I do for you and experience you in this way.

You're like no other woman I have had the pleasure to please. You're allowing yourself to be vulnerable enough to go places even I have never observed before. So don't think I feel you are lacking in any way. You are quite an adventure, believe me, the wildest ride in the amusement park, my lovely."

"Well that's quite a tribute, Robert. I'm glad you're so amused." His observation does nothing to alleviate my distress; he again avoids my inquiry. "Oh, you definitely do me. But *we* haven't done it, not together. Will we? Can we?"

"Yes." That's his clipped answer. He gets up and I sense he is now irritated. Something in his energy feels way off now and I don't know what it is or what to do about it. We shower together downstairs and dress for our hike without much conversation. I sense he does not want to discuss this. I'm forced to let it go, for now at least.

Taking a detour through town for coffee, he wants me to meet a couple of his good friends. We stop at a Starbucks located inside a supermarket, which surprises me. I guess I expected that he'd have a favorite local café where he met with his friends, but apparently not. He's quite animated, introducing me to Joe, the barista, and Ralph, the assistant manager of the store. He tells them where I'm from, where we dined last night and what our plans are for the day. He makes a point to put his arm around me, winking at them and kissing me on the forehead. They smile indulgently and are friendly, in a service provider-to-patron sort of way, not disingenuous, but not like real friends at all. And that's it. We purchase our coffees and pastries and leave. These are the people he considers his close friends? I am baffled.

We head for the hills in silence, his earlier animation now subdued. He clearly doesn't want to talk. I have questions about many things. Not just about the way things are going with us but things I wanted to know about him, his life, Sedona, the magic. I don't ask. It's a glorious day and I have my camera and a coffee and am able to shift into the moment. Strolling leisurely up a winding trail, he describes various flora and fauna, what to notice, what to avoid, local history, and how to spot the naturally heart-shaped red clay rocks that are scattered everywhere. It's almost as if he sensed some of my ponderings. I'm also thinking about his solitariness and wonder if he's lonely.

"What do you and your friends like to do together, Robert? Do they enjoy hiking with you?"

He says they never do anything together but he sees them every day about the same time for coffee. Then he picks up the pace, putting just enough distance between us to make conversation difficult. Who are the *they* he is referring to? I don't ask.

We spend hours walking, taking pictures from rocky outcroppings, listening to the wind. Sitting on one very comfortable rock, shaped like an easy chair, I wonder about all the tales I've heard of Sedona's vortex and special energy. There is definitely something ethereal about the peace and serenity I am feeling in my heart and mind, but is it because of the energy of Sedona or is it due to the incredible sexual release and satisfaction that I'm experiencing within my body? I decide it must be a combination of both. What a blessing and an adventure to be provided with such exquisite pleasure.

Heading back down only when we get hungry, we cruise into town again for a quick lunch at a sidewalk café. On the way back to his home he suggests we stop at a small Catholic church embedded in the side of a monument, looking out at the famous Cathedral formations. I don't remember ever having a discussion of any depth about our faith or religious persuasions. He leaves me to sit alone in the stillness of this small, ultra-modern chapel, meditating on a simple cross and a statue of Our Lady in front of full-length windows overlooking the valley of monuments. Outside, he chats with tourists. Later, I ask him if being Jewish made him feel uncomfortable in a Catholic parish.

"Being Jewish means feeling uncomfortable no matter what. Churches and synagogues are for the devout, which I am not.

In fact, I don't give a fuck about religion, yours, mine or anyone else's." I let his rant dissipate in the wind. Now it is I who doesn't feel like talking. I'm enjoying the serenity I feel in my body, the lovely ache of muscles used exploring those trails as well as the sense of that other something I felt up there in the hills and again in this parish.

Once back home, he heads to his computer closet. I strip off my clothes and lay in the late afternoon sun, drifting, dreaming in the quiet solitude of his back patio enclosed with rock and desert plantings. After a while he stands at the door and calls for me to come in. "You're starting to burn, lovely. We don't want that. This sun, even in late afternoon is more intense than you realize. Come in, please." I move to the shady front deck swing and continue drifting in and out of reverie. Sometime later, he comes to sit with me. Within seconds, he's fondling me, playing with my body.

"Robert, please, not right now."

"Again, what you say and what you want are not in synch are they?"

"Yes, in fact, they are. I am completely content and am enjoying this quiet. Can't we save this for later please?"

"I'm afraid not. Let me demonstrate why."

I don't know how he does it or why his touch has such an implosive sexual impact on me, but when he focuses his attention on me and touches me the way he does, my libido lurches to life. I had no desire or interest at all just one second before, but now his lips and fingers begin to perform their miracles. He can make me come before I even utter a protest. It's really delicious and it's really disconcerting. My will evaporates and I'm completely at his mercy begging for more.

"I rest my case. Cock-a-doodle-doo, my lovely." he whispers, standing abruptly returning to his computer, leaving me in mid-orgasm, undone once again in this weird one-sided arrangement.

"Robert, come back please."

"Can't get enough, can you? You're quite insatiable." He chuckles from his enclave.

"Robert, please, I want to talk to you."

"Are you sure that's what you want?" He appears behind the swing and musses my already tangled hair.

"Yes. Please sit down." He sits next to me warily, as men do when women tell them they need to talk. Turning to face him, I drape my arms around his neck. His body tenses and his half smile fades to suspicious concern. "Doctor Robert, I feel you withdrawing from me now even as I reach out to connect with you. I don't understand and I want you to tell me why you won't let me reciprocate my affection for you. You've so generously bestowed pleasures upon me and I am not complaining. But it's so unbalanced. I want to please you too."

"We've already talked about this. You do please me. I am pleased pleasing you, Savannah. There is nothing left to discuss."

I want to find a way to connect with him on our last night together. He wants to go back into town for dinner. Clearly the Doctor is not willing to engage in a conversation that's important to me. I can't find a way in.

"We'll go to Takashi for some lovely seafood and saké and discuss where and when we'll meet next," he interjects impatiently.

"Why don't I prepare a simple meal for us here? I can assemble something tasty from whatever you have on hand."

"I don't keep much food here as you may have noticed. I prefer dining out. I have my favorite haunts in town and I like to support them. We'll eat at Takashi."

In that moment, I realize we haven't had even one meal here all weekend. Not even a juice or coffee. I feel disoriented again. Why had I not noticed this before? It's unlike me to be so nonobservant. Is this Sedona's mysterious spell, or his?

"I don't want to get dressed and drive back to town." I complain.

"Don't get dressed then, lovely, but we'll eat in town."

I give in to the fact that Robert is addicted to making his rounds and as his guest, tagging along with him is expected—required—especially if I intend to eat, which I must do soon. I suddenly realize how hungry I am.

"Fine, Robert. I can see that you don't want to discuss something I consider important, so we won't. I give up. Let's talk about where we might meet next. How about a beach town in southern California? I like Santa Barbara."

"We can do that but considering the fact that you're so loud, crying out and yelping like a coyote when you climax, it might be more prudent and private to meet here again. How do you feel about a return visit?"

"I'm loud?" Except for that one yelp, I can't remember making a sound above a gasp or whimper. We haven't even descended into an animated argument of any volume as yet. "Hmm. So I'm too loud for the beach. Well then, what about a mountain retreat? Maybe Tahoe or Taos?" He trails me into the bathroom while I finish dressing, wraps his arms around my waist as I attempt to untangle my hair and find my lipstick.

"Are you not comfortable here, Savannah?" Is he? This beautiful house has no more personal feeling than any resort we might visit. We could be anywhere. "I like the way you look right now. Don't do a thing to your hair or face. You look refreshed and relaxed. Why aren't you comfortable here?"

"I am thoroughly enjoying myself here, as you must have noticed." His body is pressed too close against me and more, he's pressing me with his intense and insistent energy. He feels different. The change makes me uncomfortable and wary.

It's so strange how this man is capable of pleasuring me in ways I wouldn't have expected and haven't experienced before. Prior to this weekend, that fact would have been difficult to comprehend. I enjoy sex. I love it. But sex is sex. Sometimes it's fabulous, sometimes it's wonderful, and sometimes it's just good enough. I wouldn't bother with anyone I didn't think was at least good enough. This time is all of that in a different way. The fact of his puny size and impotence coupled with his excellent compensatory skills has made this adventure all about me. That's unexpected and fun for a change but sharing love, affection and sexuality is much more important to me. I realize now how much I need that for fulfillment. We aren't making love or even just having sex, not together. I'm not exactly sure what to call what we are doing.

"Well?" He asks again.

"Well what?"

"You haven't answered me."

"Well, I was just thinking about one of our conversations a few weeks ago, remember? We talked about traveling."

"We'll be late for our reservation. Are you ready yet? Let's go."

In the mirror, I watch him abruptly turn and leave the room. I catch up with him as he walks out the front door. "You're leaving without me?"

"Of course not." His tension is visible and palpable, as he trundles me briskly into the car, slamming the door with unnecessary force.

He slides behind the wheel slamming his door as well and starts the car, spitting gravel as he backs out of the driveway. "What's wrong, Robert? Are you angry?"

"Of course not." He is angry. His jaw is set, hands gripping the wheel, driving too fast. "Why would I be angry?"

"Are you?" He is. I have no idea why, but he is.

"Why don't you want to come back here? Isn't Sedona beautiful enough for you? Haven't I provided you with exactly what I said I would? Have you had to do anything at all that did not please you?"

"What's this all about Robert? I didn't say I wouldn't come back here. Sedona is beautiful and you are a wonderfully gracious host as I have told you several times. What's the problem?"

"The problem is that I make specific suggestions or recommendations to you and you don't give the slightest consideration to them or to what I might want."

"What *do* you want? Several weeks ago you mentioned traveling and meeting in other locales. That was your idea, not mine, although I like it. And what do you mean I haven't had to do anything displeasing. Why would I?"

He drives in stony silence, ignoring me until we arrive in town. Instead of opening my door as he has been, he walks briskly into the small Japanese restaurant leaving me in the car. This excessive overreaction to a simple conversation distresses me. I lose my appetite. I sit.

He reappears, opening my door. "Well?" Taking my arm determinedly as I climb out of the car, he practically pulls me into the restaurant.

"What the hell, Robert?"

"Savannah, don't be peevish. Let's not spend our last evening in a sulk." He gives the server our order without consulting the menu. "No arguments?"

"None."

"Then may I assume that finally one of my recommendations suits you and that you will enjoy the miso soup, soft shell crab and asparagus tempura? Or are you simply peevish by nature?"

"Where do you come up with these words? I am being polite. I am being considerate. I am making an attempt to be sensitive to what you say you want."

"That's my line, Savannah. And you have it all wrong. I am a slave to your desire but I am not your servant, a cue you have missed completely."

"What are we talking about now, Doctor? What cue have I missed?"

"You missed the cue that an affectionate reciprocity in our case, may not be like for like. For instance I'd enjoy a bit of heated aggression from you. In fact I'll admit that the thought thrills me.

I am well aware that you have a dominating nature but you have chosen a more submissive stance this weekend. You might consider my desires and allow me the pleasure of a little restraint, the satisfaction of a pinch, a bite, or spanking, perhaps a mild whipping."

"A whipping? You want me to hurt you?" What the…?!

"No need to draw blood. I abhor violence." Is he serious?

"Robert! Damn it! The mere suggestion of violence, particularly any kind of sexual violence, upsets me. It is not in my repertoire." I feel queasy. Missed cues? Dominating nature? Mild whippings? I feel sick.

We stare at each other. The food is served and I can't bring myself to touch it. "Come now, Savannah. You need to eat to maintain your stamina."

"Why didn't you tell me this before, Robert? I would never have suspected this of you, especially since you have been so gentle with me."

"Of course I am gentle with you. That is what you want, at least this time. What I want for myself is something else. We'll resume this discussion later." What does that mean: what I want, at least this time?

He ate his meal in silence while I poked and pushed mine around the plate with the chopsticks. Everything has changed. I'm now sitting with a different person than the one I thought I was coming to know. He's revealing what he wants from me—something I am not capable of delivering—and is gauging my reaction. I didn't see this coming.

Earlier, we had talked about strolling around town, doing a little shopping tonight after dinner. I have no enthusiasm for that now. But Doctor Robert has decided. Once he plans to do something it's on the agenda and I realize at last that I have little hope of influencing him otherwise. His arm draped over my shoulder, he tows me around the corner to a small courtyard of shops.

"Robert, I really don't feel like shopping right now. I'm not at all sure how I feel. I don't know how to respond to what you've just told me. I think you've misjudged me. I don't see how you can expect me to want to hurt you. I don't want to hurt you. I can't do it."

"Hurting is relative wouldn't you say? There are times when a little pain can be quite stimulating. Done with the right intention it can be very erotic." He stopped abruptly in front of a shop window displaying dresses and wraps. "Look at this red dress, do you like it? I can see you in this, it's perfect for you. I'd like to buy this for you as a parting gesture, a gift you can model for me tonight. I will relish peeling it slowly from your body and . . . "

"Robert, knock it off. How can you suddenly be so insensitive? Your behavior and revelation confuse me. We are talking about your pleasure in experiencing pain. This is something I don't understand at all. And I don't give a damn about the dress."

"Come now, Savannah. You are overreacting rather dramatically, wouldn't you say? You'll look lovely in this dress. Red is your color. I want to buy it for you, feel your body through the silk, see your breasts peeking out from this plunging neckline, touch them, undress you slowly, and taste you one last time this weekend. Let's go in so you can try it on for me."

"Fuck you, Robert."

He kisses my neck, even as I resist and pushes me into the shop with his hand on my ass. "Stop it, Robert. Is this the end of the discussion?" He laughs and slides his hand between my legs, quickly rubbing my crotch before waving to the shopkeeper and pointing to the red dress in the window. "Robert, damn it. Damn you. Let's go. Please."

"Size 8, I believe. Isn't that right, my lovely?"

Damn him. I feel that strange exhaustion creep over me again as I realize that I am at his mercy. I don't want a scene. I consider the dress with minimal interest, sigh and relent. "Yes, size 8, thank you." The salesgirl leads me to a changing room and hands me the dress. I stare into the mirror, wondering, what the bloody hell now?

"What's taking you so long? Come out and show me." Robert calls to me. I stand naked in front of the mirror staring at the dress I've dropped on the floor, feeling disoriented and well, peeved. I zip it up and am pissed that the damn thing fits me perfectly. When he sees me in it, Robert is effusive, telling the girl I'll wear it and gives her his card.

"I don't want to wear it. I'm taking it off. Please wrap it for me," I mumble to the clerk.

"She'll wear it." Robert counters and wins. The girl looks at me askance. I just shrug and look away. I can't win when Robert makes up his mind. I no longer care to argue.

The dark road that winds up to his drive matches my mood. I would like to be getting on the plane right now. How can I stay with him tonight? What does he expect from me now? The man-pleasing behavior encoded in my DNA, activated by an earlier sense of obligation to reciprocate, has short-circuited into a case of dread. I haven't asked for or expected anything he wasn't more than willing to offer. I haven't actually asked him for anything except how I might please him. I wish now, with everything I am, I hadn't asked that. He's turning it on me.

Parked in the darkness we sit in silence. He's making no move to go in, so I wait miserably in my new red dress, trying to anticipate what he might decide is next. "Are you ready?" Chills shiver through my body. I'm not. "Savannah, whatever you are fabricating in your overactive imagination is likely more harrowing than anything based in reality. Stop torturing yourself. This weekend is strictly about pleasure. I am merely asking you if you are ready to go into the house."

"Robert, we appear to have opposing views on what constitutes pleasure. In all these months of talking, you never once indicated to me that your personal pleasure would require me to cause you pain. We wouldn't be sitting here right now if I had known that, would we?"

"Perhaps not. But think of what you would have missed, Savannah. Think about what we'd have both missed. I will confess that I was fairly certain you would react this way. I merely hoped you could be persuaded. I had hoped you would so enjoy yourself that just possibly you'd desire to expand beyond your comfort level, maybe even enjoy a new experience. You are a natural dominator; you just haven't discovered yourself in that role sexually yet."

"Robert, this entire weekend is a new experience for me. I've been submissive with you, but you encouraged that, dominating me completely and stopping any attempt I've made to try to please you. Now I learn that what you want is a dominatrix so you can be submissive. Can't you see how I might have missed the cue?"

"You've not only missed the cue, you've missed the point. You still seem to have no idea how it thrills me to have such an impact on you, such power over you sexually. Discovering just what makes you come undone and watching you lose control has given my dominating nature a generalized boost. And I have no inclination toward submissiveness. I simply enjoy and get off on rougher more aggressive sex play from time to time."

Oh my God. What the hell? This man with that teeny limp thing wants to ride rough? I can't even begin to visualize what that might mean with him. I wish I could just go home right now. I want to go home.

"Silence, Savannah? Hardly like you to be silent although I've come to admire your expertise in sulking."

"Fuck off, Doctor." Now I'm pissed. "You drop this stink bomb in the middle of paradise and expect me to applaud you for ruining everything? You have the heart of a terrorist."

"Now that's more like you, my lovely. Welcome back, Savannah."

Damn it. Why can't I keep my mouth shut? Encouraging him is the last thing I want to do. I stomp up to the house, frustrated and angry at myself for falling directly into the trap he has laid for me. He's baiting me to become angry and aggressive. I won't do it. I rattle the doorknob but the house is locked.

"I have the key to the house but you hold the key to whatever happens next. You have all the power. That is why I am your slave. Do you grasp the concept yet?"

"No, I do not. How is it even possible to grasp all these switchbacks? You've placed me in an untenable position and I resent it. You were minimally forthcoming with me. You were dishonest. I refuse to play your game. I have no judgment on your preferences, only that you didn't reveal them to me and now I feel as if all the pleasure you have given me has been calculated and repossessed. Thanks." Here come the tears.

"Come in, Savannah. I'm not the big bad wolf. I've told you all along that I will always respond to what you want. There may come a time when what you want is different than now, but now is now."

Confusion and frustration overwhelm me. I feel myself start to fall apart emotionally. I'm standing on his porch in this slinky red dress that I am starting to hate. I don't want to go in and I don't know what to do next. "I wanted to make love together, Robert." Stop those tears, Savannah. "It's not turning out that way." Stop them now! "We are not on the same page. I am sad and distressed about it." Stop. Now!

We climb the stairs and I drift out to the front porch and stare dejectedly at the moonlight on the monuments. He heads to his computer sanctuary. Now what? That feeling of emotional exhaustion continues to roll over me like a thick dense fog. I turn and watch him in his closet flipping through screens. He seems untouched by our drama.

"May I take a bath?"

"Of course, Savannah, you don't have to ask. I see you are disheartened. No need to be. All is as it is and was. Nothing has really changed." Yes it has, Robert. Everything has changed for me. "Have a good soak and relax. I want to make love to you the way you want tonight. You are not obligated to do anything at all that you are uncomfortable with. I thought I had made that point with clarity. This weekend is about pleasure so don't think that I have not experienced any. I have repeatedly told you how it makes me feel to be with you, the way you want. Let's not have everything that has been wonderful ruined by peevishly sulking or over-thinking."

"Whatever, Robert. I sulk, I think, I feel. And apparently I'm also loud and peevish. This is how I am and I'm drained by this emotional roller coaster ride with you."

He shrugs and turns back to his screen. I walk dejectedly toward the master bath, peeling off the red dress along the way. I drop it on the floor, then think twice about it. Picking it up, I fold it carefully in as small a bundle as I can manage and hide it under his bed. As I draw the bath a cloud covers the moon and the garden outside the windows looks haunted. I submerge to my chin. The moon reappearing casts a long eerie shadow over the huge stones. The clouds rolling across the sky give those rocks the illusion of moving toward me, closing in on me. I close my eyes and send my mind to the comfort of my own home. The warm bath is calming and I begin to feel somewhat better, somewhat resolved and resigned. Robert is a gentleman, a quirky odd character, but essentially a good man. He just won't be my man.

I realize that once again, I've been struggling to find a way to connect more closely with a man I like and thought I might want to be involved with. I also realize that in the far reaches of my mind I've been trying to overcome the obstacles presented and orchestrate a way to somehow work out a future, a partnership that would work with him even knowing full well that we could never live together for more reasons than geography. This is a habit of mine. I've been here before, bracing myself against some unexpected glitch as it reveals itself, determined to unravel the entire story. I try to pull impossible elements together and make them fit. It's an old entrenched pattern that doesn't shake loose or ever seem to change with my strongest intentions. How it could still be an unexpected occurrence is sad and disappointing to me. But I feel a bit calmer, as the truth sinks in and I resign myself to accepting and dealing with the situation as it is now.

Robert is already in bed waiting for me when I finish my bath. He gestures for me to come to him. I'm not only reticent; I involuntarily step away and start to worry again. "Please, Savannah. Come lay with me. Let me ease your mind about everything we've discussed. You have nothing to fear or worry about with me. I hope you know that by now."

I have no real reason to doubt him. I relent. I don't really want to sleep in the Giants football gift shop. We curl up together. I pray that our last hours together can be spent just like this, without pressure from him for anything more. Prayer heard and answered. We sleep, peacefully uninterrupted. But in the morning I am awakened with his face between my legs. I was sleeping so soundly that hadn't even felt him move.

"Robert, what are you doing?"

"Don't deprive me of one last slurp of your savory juice, Savannah. That would be cruel."

Here is a man, a doctor with incredibly impressive skills that cannot be explained easily. How he turns a situation, a conversation, a feeling, and in this instance, a sleepy woman who has lost all interest in any further sexual activity with him around to an immediate sensual arousal is beyond explanation. I didn't think I wanted him to touch me at all and yet he quickly coaxes me to an easy climax with just his mouth, ending our weekend on that sweet note expecting nothing in return. It's just weird.

I packed as he showered. We stopped at Starbucks as prescribed, listened to Eva Cassidy sing "Over the Rainbow" again on the way out of town and held hands nearly all the way to the airport. I'm not sure how to talk about any plans for future rendezvous and he doesn't seem inclined to broach the subject. I begin to feel that an unspoken understanding, a mutual agreement has been reached and we part with a friendly, even affectionate, acceptance. I'm grateful for that.

As I settle into my seat on the plane reflecting on these last few days and the chance I took in coming here, I have no regret. It's been an excellent adventure. I was the object of his delicious skills and attention. But after last night's revelation, I realize this weekend is all we can ever have together. He calls me just before I turn off my phone for takeoff.

"Have a good trip home, Savannah. Cock-a-doodle-doo, my lovely."

"Doodle-doodle-do, Doctor, and thank you, for everything.

Love thy neighbor -- but don't get caught.
 ~ Anonymous

The Man in the Middle

or me, traveling was once an exciting and enjoyable adventure. No more, if I have to fly. Since terrorism came into vogue, the entire process of flying—from arriving and parking at the airport, to the shakedown at security or dealing with customs, to overbooked flights with passengers crammed into impossibly close proximity—has become as exciting and enjoyable as a hemorrhoid. Arriving at my destination as quickly and safely as possible is my goal and only consolation.

My late night flight from Los Angeles to Seattle is delayed boarding, delayed taking off, and packed so tightly in coach, which is the only ticket I could arrange, that it's not possible to avoid touching shoulders with the large man seated in the middle. I'm tucked in next to the window, leaning against it for the illusion of personal space.

We wait, the plane idling in the long queue on the runway. The feeling of discomfort and impatience among the passengers and crew is palpable and disturbs me. I'm not the only one fidgeting and squirming, trying to adjust to the cramped space. The cabin's stifling recycled air mingles with passengers' stale exhales. A small smelly dog whining in its carrier is shoved under the seat behind me and hollering babies, being shushed by their harried mothers, occupy the tail section, just a few rows back.

When at last we are able to take off and are in the air, the beverage cart is a more than welcome distraction. I can't think what to order, but I'm certain I want more than one. The flight attendant finally appears at our aisle and the man in the middle orders a whisky soda, settling my quandary. I order three. She hands me my little saviors with a raised eyebrow and a practiced weary smile. I knock back the first in three swallows and take a deep breath. The man in the middle sips his cocktail, briefly glancing at me with amused curiosity before opening his newspaper. My two remaining drinks I hold securely, one in each hand. Slowly, methodically, I sip from each alternately, willing them to last and do what they're intended to: settle me so that I can deal with the next few hours of this aggravating journey.

When the empty cups are collected and the lights finally dimmed, I feel sufficiently calmed and curl into the tiny pillow tucked against the window hoping to sleep, though I am rarely able to achieve that on a plane. My fellow passengers are quieting down as well, and although the three whiskeys have definitely helped to numb my busy mind and relax me, there is no escaping the compacted situation with the large man filling the space in the middle.

He is big, wide, tall and substantial ... not fat ... just huge. I wonder how he can sit so placidly, squeezed into his seat with his knees pressed tightly against the back of the one in front of him. His arm and elbow spilling over the armrest between us make it impossible for me to move even a fraction of an inch without touching him. His demeanor is quiet and resigned; his only movements the adjusting of his glasses and turning the pages of his paper.

I cannot get comfortable. I am unable to rest and then, to my dismay, discover that I need to use the lavatory. Damn it. Contemplating the logistics required to accomplish this feat only serves to reactivate my aggravation. I'm going to have to climb over the knees of the man packed in the middle because the woman sprawled in the aisle seat is sound asleep and snoring.

Unbuckling, I struggle to stand and ponder how to make this move, let alone make it without disturbing him. He notices my hesitation, folds his newspaper neatly and does his best to spread his legs so that I can step between his knees and get past him, but we get tangled up anyway and I fall onto him before finally squeezing past the sleeping woman. When I return, we repeat this process of awkward forced intimacy. I fucking hate to fly these days.

Struggling to find a comfortable position, I try in vain to refrain from wiggling one way or squirming the other. I know I'm disrupting this poor man next to me, although he is graciously accommodating and making an effort to commiserate with me through shrugs and expressions of empathy. I finally give up on trying not to touch him and brace myself upright, which means shoulder against shoulder. He turns toward me briefly and smiles with an understanding nod, then resumes reading his paper.

The plane is mostly darkened now except for his reading light on, directly above me. The battery in my iPod has gone dead, a baby screams somewhere in the back, I'm starting to get a headache, I want to sleep but can't, and I am utterly and completely pissed.

The man in the middle folds his paper, takes off his glasses and places them neatly into his vest pocket before finally turning off his light. Covering himself as best he can with his tweed jacket, unable to avoid jostling me, he reclines his seat, closes his eyes and sits motionless. This annoys me even more. He must be so much more uncomfortable than I am, and yet he appears able to adjust himself to the situation with ease. I add this to my list of grievances as one more example of life's niggling injustices.

The plane is quiet now, the crew attending only to random call lights, and there's no sound but the droning thrum of the engines. It's past midnight and almost everyone is sleeping, everyone except me. I remember the soft lemon-colored cashmere wrap I'd thought to bring and reach into the bag under my feet to retrieve it, inadvertently bumping and poking the calves of the man in the middle. I feel cozier, but nothing helps me fall asleep.

Eventually the idea occurs to me, that since it's dark and I'm covered, I could touch and comfort myself to release my tension, as I am prone to do whenever I can't sleep. No one would be the wiser. Under my shawl, I pull up my skirt a little, move my panties aside and begin a familiar soothing communication with my tender moist private parts. Maybe it's the whiskey or the drone of the engines or maybe it's the fun of pleasuring myself in secret. I don't know and it doesn't matter to me, because I become very aroused very quickly. In this intimately confined space, I realize that the ticklish challenge will be to kindle an orgasm without moving too overtly or making any revealing sounds. Fun. No one is paying any attention to me and I begin to lose myself in my dreamy sensual escape. In the process, I find myself leaning against the man in the middle, although he doesn't appear to notice.

My shoulder against the warmth and rhythmic breathing of the man in the middle momentarily diverts my attention to him and I have a sudden wicked impulse. I lay my left hand on his thigh and he stirs just slightly. With my right hand I stimulate myself to the first shivering little orgasm. As one quickly evolves into another, I slide my hand over the man in the middle's crotch. He opens his eyes with a start and stares straight ahead. I'm smiling for more than one reason now. He doesn't move. My breathing comes faster. He glances at me, and catching my eye, quickly turns away, closing his eyes again. Under his jacket, I feel his cock harden against his slacks. His breath catches as he realizes what I'm doing, but he doesn't stop me.

I stroke his bulging crotch and he lets out a little gasp. Carefully undoing his belt and lowering his zipper, I find his penis peeping through his boxers and touch him. His entire body stiffens, his jaw clenches. He doesn't stop me. I decide his compliance is an invitation and begin to run my fingers along his shaft, gently massaging that tender spot under his sensitive tip. He sits straight up, alert now, his hand reaching tentatively under my soft wrap, then clutches my thigh tightly as I fondle him. I yank my skirt up under my shawl, so that his hand is pulled further up my leg and slips onto the bare warm skin near the top of my thigh. He turns and stares at me then, his eyes wide with surprise and confusion. I can feel him struggling to maintain control, his breath heavy but he makes no sound. He looks straight ahead again, closing his grey brown eyes tightly.

The first little drips of pre-cum escape him, offering my fingers the lubrication they need to finish him off. Stroking his cock more vigorously, I reach further within myself, my fingers stirring up another orgasm. He covers my busy hand with his now, following the way I move and touch myself. The tip of his thumb rests lightly, unintentionally, on my clit, his hand tentative but heavy atop mine. He hesitates, perhaps unsure of his role, so I offer some instruction. I slip my fingers out, guiding his long middle finger into my silky furrow. I lay my hand on top of his, pressing his finger deeper into my naughty wetness. He has grasped the concept now, his thick long finger exploring my slippery depths, inadvertently discovering my deep hot spot. I climax in shock and pleasure, contracting around his startled fucking finger. He feels me and pulses, his cum squirts with force. He groans, quickly covering his mouth with his other hand. I moan, watching him struggle to contain himself. It's thrilling.

The big man in the middle is visibly shaken, his eyes and lips clamped tightly shut. I'm giddy, scarcely able to restrain myself from laughing out loud. As we both slow our breathing and begin to collect ourselves, I gently tuck his dick back into his dampened pants and zip him up. I have to remove his paralyzed hand from my slippery crotch and place it under his jacket, before I can pull my panties back into place. At last he relaxes and lays his head back, a broad smile spreading across his face. I turn toward the window, wondering what the hell had gotten into me, and giggle at the nasty fun of it all. Not one word has been spoken.

In time, the captain turns on the seatbelt sign and announces the beginning of our descent into Seattle. I steal a glance at the man in the middle and discover that he's silently chuckling, his eyes still closed, and I giggle at our conspiracy. When the plane reaches the gate and everyone begins the customary frantic gathering of bags and belongings, the woman in the aisle seat awakens, wipes a thread of drool from the corner of her mouth and stands abruptly. She leans over the man in the middle, who remains seated, clutching his tweed jacket, re-arranging it over the dark damp stain on the crotch of his slacks.

"Honey, get up. I need help reaching my bag."

He steals a glance, sees me smiling and winks.

Flying, I decide with a naughty grin, has once again become an exciting and enjoyable adventure.

Pleasure is Nature's test, her sign of approval.
  ~ Oscar Wilde

Pleasure as a Higher Calling

Johnny and I were lovers once—passionate, avid, insatiable lovers. One day he changed his mind, had a change of heart, and changed the story. He said he needed time to think, needed space, needed to process, needed to assess the impact we were having on each other's lives, needed to think about the future, all the usual things we say to someone when we want to create distance, when we're headed for the back door.

After the intense intimacy we shared, it was odd to end so abruptly, almost as strange as how quickly we fell in together, but even more surprising was that I didn't miss him more. I loved having sex with him and he definitely meant more to me than a mere distraction. Still, I hadn't fallen *in love* with him, and he wasn't *in love* with me. He wanted to go. I had no choice. I let him go and let go too. I became philosophical about it. We've stayed loosely in touch with emails, but we hadn't had any contact for a while until yesterday, when I received this message from him:

"Hey Savannah, read this . . . 'cause if these facts are true . . . *'Sex can reduce a fever because of the sweat produced. Sex is also a pain reliever, ten times more effective than Valium: immediately before orgasm, levels of the hormone oxytocin rise by five times, triggering a huge release of endorphins. These chemicals enhance the immune system and generate a sense of wellness. They can also calm pain, from a minor headache to migraine to arthritis, and with no negative secondary effects. Migraines can disappear because the pressure in the brain's blood vessels is lowered while having an orgasm. So, a woman's headache is a good reason for having sex and should be encouraged, not the opposite.'*

. . . then having sex with you should cure cancer."

That post had circulated on Facebook all week, why is he bothering to forward something like this now? It's typical of the mixed signals he sent me toward the end of our love affair. He'd cancel something we'd planned to do together with the excuse that he had to work, then spend all day sexting me with long threads of erotic banter. What is he up to? Is this meant to be a joke, a compliment, a come-on, a reconnect? Does he miss me? I decided it was all of that and at the same time nothing.

We'd had many intimate conversations and in the heat of our sex made some vulnerable confessions. Some, I knew, he wished he hadn't. Me too, but that was over now. He hadn't responded with much enthusiasm lately to my overtures to stay connected, so I decided to ignore this attempt on his part. But thoughts of him, memories of the yummy sex and fun we'd had kept tickling their way into my day and later in the afternoon I just had to reply to his message.

"Cute, Johnny. You might enjoy learning that the electric meter for my house ran backwards whenever we were generating. P.S. Energy sent me a refund check. We could have made a dent in dependency on foreign oil, sugar . . . or minimally powered the Puget Sound grid . . . just saying . . ."

"That's for damn sure, darlin' . . . 'cause you know . . . whenever I climbed into my rig to go back home after being with you, the tank was somehow full again."

"No need to speculate on crude, handsome dude. Wall Street weeps. There are so many pleasurable benefits to organic power generation, don'cha think?"

We could play and tease each other and I enjoyed that too, but why were we doing it now? It made me miss him. I dropped the thread.

* * * * * * * * * *

One morning, back when Johnny and I were still generating intense power and heat, we were engaged in a lively discussion about sex, specifically orgasms and energy production. He had just observed how, by some miracle of anatomy, sex that would be pretty straightforward with anyone else happened to end up being incredible with us. He was musing how it surprised him, because no matter how many times we made love—and we did that quite a lot—it stayed fresh and continued to thrill us. I was trailing him from the bedroom to the kitchen, wanting to add my perspective on the importance and the significance of the sexuality that we enjoyed together.

"Sugar . . . since you have so generously contributed to and infinitely enhanced my pleasures, I have decided to share a little secret with you."

"Savannah, we both know it's not possible for you to keep a secret. You're uncensored. Every thought in your busy mind and every stirring in your hot body gets expressed. What are you gonna tell me that you haven't already?"

That statement was so Johnny. Everything he thought, said, and did had the same sequence. The beginning: he has an experience. A middle: he decides something about it, right, wrong or ridiculous. Then an ending: that's it, it's final, end of inquiry, end of further possibility. Somehow that didn't detract from the fact that he was one of the best, most sexually intuitive lovers I've ever known. I wasn't interested in wasting even one delicious minute wondering if there was a dichotomy in any of it.

"Are you interested in hearing my perspective or not? And even if you aren't, would you kindly consider indulging me anyway?"

Just minutes ago I had made him writhe in ecstasy by awakening him with that slow sensuous blowjob I knew he was dreaming about. Surprise, Johnny. I know lots of things, especially about you. I don't tell you everything.

"Hey . . . sarcasm is my job around here. Yes, enlighten me . . . please . . . as if you could be stopped." He laughed. He laughed, but I knew that if he could get away with ignoring me right now he would. He couldn't.

"Johnny, even though you are such an accomplished smart-ass, I still feel there is the remote possibility that you could experience a few brief moments of enlightenment. It won't hurt a bit."

"Darlin', anything . . . everything you say and do regarding sex is interesting to me. Go ahead, enlighten me." He kissed my cheek and opened the fridge.

"Oh Johnny. It's a good thing you're so cute. It's your saving grace." I pressed my body against his back, kissed his neck, squeezed his ass and wrapped my arms around his waist, while he studied the contents of the fridge. "I think it's like this," I said, laying my cheek on his back, collecting the thoughts that had rushed over me this morning as I awakened. "I believe the reason that I covet our sexuality, and have become so orgasmic, has to do with my own particular service to humanity, as I have come to understand it."

"Oh my God." He groaned. "It's early, Savannah. We haven't even had breakfast, damn."

"Hey, you said you'd listen." I pouted.

"Ok, darlin', I'm listening, you've got my attention." He half turned in my arms and pecked me on the cheek again before continuing his examination of the meat and cheese drawer.

"Just let me finish before I forget what I was thinking." I reorganized my thoughts. "So . . . if I am to continue to be an energetic catalyst, a beacon, a bright light on the path for others, which I believe is my calling, then I must keep my orgasmic reserves filled at all times." It sounded silly, even to me, so I couldn't keep from grinning, but I meant it. "I know my energy is naturally attracting anyway and many people feel better just being around me, but especially so if I subtly cloak myself in the sweet feeling tone of orgasmic pleasure." Expressing this thought out loud made me giggle with delight.

Turning to fully face me now, rolling his eyes, he smirked, "How noble and weirdly arrogant of you. A cloak of orgasms? Jesus, what the hell are you talking about?"

"Sugar, don't you feel uplifted like I do when we're here doing what we do so well together? When we generate energy like we were last night and this morning, you also hold that high vibration, that tone of pleasure. You're holding it right now. Can't you sense it? Can't you feel what I'm talking about?"

"Well yeah . . . I guess so . . . I hadn't thought about how I was feeling in exactly those terms . . . or any terms . . . I think I'm starving."

We were both hungry and in need of a breakfast, having finally climbed out of bed after a long night of pleasure-making and a morning of delicious arousals. I pointed out that he had started the conversation. It was he who observed that we never seemed to run out of energy when it comes to making love, having sex. It was he who had brought it to my attention this morning and inspired me to contemplate how and why all that worked so well with us.

"This is what making love can do for us, Johnny. Making love, by its very nature, is co-creative and re-generating. Exerting our energy on sex deeply satisfies us in the moment and leaves us delightfully spent but for some reason, never drained afterwards. I think the reason for me is that I purposefully absorb the essence of those moments of unbearably yummy pleasure. I love to drench myself in the delectable sensuality of that feeling. I want to capture the energy of our lovemaking and orgasms and pull it in so deeply that it becomes a part of my own essence. Then I hold it, preserve it, store it and retrieve it for my own health and well-being and also for my lover. That's you, sugar. And later, when I want to or need to, I can access that essence of pleasure, that energy now mingled with mine, and extend the tone of it to others."

"Hmm . . . you might be right. Making love with you is delicious, it's fun and yeah . . . it's energizing. I guess I hadn't really thought about it." He opened the freezer and poked through some packages before slamming it shut again. "Exactly what are we talking about here? What kind of voodoo are you performing on me? And, damn it, darlin', what do we have to eat?"

"I'm not doing anything to you. We're doing something together. But here's how I feel it works: as a service to others, when I'm drenched in this juicy higher love vibration, whoever I come into contact with—and that includes you—feels elevated. Others may not know why they feel better, or maybe it's lighter, just being around me. They may not relate it to me. And it's not really expressed or received in any sexual way. It's just an elevated vibration and feeling tone. And when we're both cloaked in this yummyness, we could be just walking down the street. Hey Johnny, let's try this today so you'll see what I mean. Someone brushing against us may simply feel better, and we'll sense it. Someone may walk past us and feel a relief, as if a burden lifted, but not know why. Or people in the grocery line or cafe will just naturally gravitate to us. I like to think of having great sex—making life-affirming love—as serving the greater global good."

"Jesus . . . now you're over the edge. Serving the greater global good? With sex? What the hell are you talking about?" He was hungry and becoming annoyed, vigorously opening and closing cabinets. I was losing my hold on the scant attention he had afforded me.

"How do you feel right now?" I tickled his ribs and forced him to turn to face me. "We fucked our brains out all night, shouldn't you be exhausted? Shouldn't I? We're hungry . . . we're starving. We need sustenance, but we're not tired."

"Hmmm. You're a strange one. And you're right. I'm *not* tired. I *am* starving. OK, wow, now I get it. You're brilliant! You're psychic! Give me a kiss, please. Then help me rustle up something for breakfast." He was leveling his sarcasm at the inside of the refrigerator again. I wondered if he was considering my point of view at all, even as he ridiculed it. I know what's true for me. I just wanted to broaden his awareness of what's possible for him, if he'd let me.

"I'll cut that papaya there and you can scramble some eggs." I offered. "Do you want toast or a muffin? How about juice? Coffee? I want coffee please. What else would you like?" I asked him as he loaded my arms with the fruit, muffins and juice.

"I want you, darlin', unless you've got some sausage." he chuckled to himself, as he broke some eggs into a dish, whipped them to a froth and poured them into a pan of melting butter.

"You're all the sausage I can handle at the moment, sugar." I meant that with honest sincerity, and gave his sausage a little yank while he cooked.

We sat across from each other at the kitchen table, beneath it our feet snuggling cozily together. I had bought some bright orange and pink tulips and arranged them in a colorful vase, hoping to encourage spring. Outside, the wind was bitter cold and grey rain was battering the windows. I was thankful that we were tucked inside and warm as we ate quietly, occasionally catching each other's eye and grinning. I was fascinated watching him wolf down his breakfast and pile more onto his plate. He winked and blew me a kiss from those lips I can never get enough of. I tingled in spite of myself.

Those twinkling blue eyes of his as well as all the rest of his pleasuring endowments, were just one more reminder of how grateful I was for our mutual exploration and generation of sexual energy. I liked to think we were compatible in other ways that counted as well. He's smart, but like most guys, he isn't thrilled to delve too deep, too often. He reached across the small table, lifted my hand to his lips and told me I was the most beautiful in the morning when I had that tousled *just fucked* look.

"Thank you, sugar . . . I think." I am completely aware that men and women's minds run along different channels, different patterns of thought. So, even though we were primarily focused on sex this morning and to be honest, almost always, he has also satisfied me intellectually, emotionally and conversationally many times . . . most of the time. I was intent on this being one of those times even though he wasn't. "Johnny, I'd like to thank you, and also honor you, for your service to humanity," I said softly, putting down my fork, suddenly overcome by affection for him.

"Huh? Me? Service to humanity? You got the wrong guy." He spread more cream cheese and apricot jam on his muffin, then said, with his mouth full, "The greater global good is your domain, darlin'. I'm out to get what I can. I'm out to get what's mine while I can. I'm not about altruism. I should be driving a Jag by now." He laughed loudly at his own joke, stuffing his mouth with the last bit of food on his plate.

"Johnny, even if you don't realize what a tender, humble servant to humanity you really are, I do. That's what I'm thanking you for . . . your tender, yummy servicing of me . . . this local little filament of humankind. You're the best, sugar."

"Thanks ... I think ... but the pleasure is mine." I had recaptured his attention, but he was staring at me with an odd expression I wasn't sure how to interpret. I continued anyway.

"You're welcome, sugar. Seriously, Johnny, it's your awareness that I want to honor now, possibly a bit prematurely, but in the event and with hope that one day you develop some." He laughed. "You can laugh, but the fact of the matter is that your sexual prowess has ignited and fanned my fire so intensely, that I not only may enjoy the most luscious ongoing body rush, I am also able to extend that higher love energy to others, as a continuing gift to the world, of course."

"You're a trip, Savannah. Do you seriously believe this shit? I mean seriously? What are you darlin'... a goddess ... some kind of mystic ... or have you gone nuts?"

"At last! You finally noticed that I'm a Goddess. I might be a mystic, sugar, but I'm not nuts." I laughed, but felt like I needed to hurry and continue, which bothered me. I could feel something subtly shift in him, and I wanted to keep it light so he didn't balk, at least too much.

"Hey, I don't have to believe it. I feel it. I experience it. I know that if I can keep my vibration held high it serves others. That's all. I observe others and notice how they feel, see how I can help and how they benefit. For me this makes having sex that much better . . . altruistic . . . a service to humanity . . . everyone benefits. But, like I've tried to explain, ultimately, it's not the energy of sexuality that others experience from me. It's more an openness and willingness to connect in an honest, authentic and accepting way. Sex can ignite the passion of that for me, within me, but it isn't really about sex at all. I don't have to actually have sex to feel this way, or to do that. I don't actually need you for this."

"Thanks again . . . I think."

"You're welcome. And I do thank you, Johnny. Because with you, I have so fully and intimately experienced sexual ecstasy, that when I focus on the feeling of it, when I imagine it, I can generate it from memory and the residual effect is basically the same. But, Johnny sugar, in the right here and now, you jump my juice and deliver the goods. You've brought me the most delicious gifts of pleasure. That's why I love sex and especially sex with you. It not only thrills me beyond description, but my bliss calls me to a higher purpose." I noticed the expression on his face had changed again and I could feel a new wave of sarcasm building behind his amused grin. "What is your bliss calling to you this morning, sugar?"

"Hmmm . . . my bliss . . . let's see . . . my bliss is still hungry and is hoping you will come over here right now so it can nibble on you some more. My bliss wants your bliss to take its hand and lead it to the promised land. My bliss doesn't really understand what the hell your bliss is talking about, but it admires itself in your reflection. My bliss loves to fuck your bliss. My bliss is begging you to come back to bed with me. Now. And jump my juice too."

He's fun. He can play. His eyes are sparkling and he's playing now. Still, I hoped that on some level he grasped the concept that I was trying to convey and that it might even be sinking into his consciousness. We usually related so easily together, but this was the first time I'd ever waxed so philosophically with him. It may have provoked a tipping point. Maybe it's what ultimately put him off, even though I'd been trying to inject my heartfelt epiphany with some humor. Maybe he could no longer take me seriously, if ever he had. It was the last time we talked like that. After that morning, it became clear to me that he was making an effort to keep our conversations light, even superficial.

The bed was where he liked to communicate best. Pillow talk was how he let his tender heart connect with mine. The bed was where we communed. The bed was where we generated power. It's where we ran the meter backwards. It's where his tank got filled. My bed served as a power base station, at least for that sweet while. Johnny changed his mind and pulled the plug. He took his yummy supercharged sausage and went home. Sometimes I really miss that, miss him, but he has his own destiny to figure out, as do I. Other lovers await us.

And I have decided that, with or without a lover, it is my calling, my *noblesse oblige*, to sustain and demonstrate orgasmic bliss to the best of my ability. Pursuing and proclaiming Pleasure as a Higher Calling has become my *raison d'être*. It has eased my own suffering and confusion and staved off caving into despair over how loveless the world has become and how alone and disconnected so many people feel. And although I am aware that some people prefer to remain entrenched in familiar habits of separation, pathos and bitterness, I know that bitterness and pleasure are mutually exclusive. I prefer pleasure.

For myself, holding that tone of pure pleasure is the cure for what ails, not only me, but also the social and relational problems we humans continue to create and perpetuate for ourselves. It is my avocation. What if everyone on earth beamed the bliss of orgasmic pleasure? I love to imagine utilizing the co-creating, co-operating, communion of orgasmic sexual energy as a generator to elevate and progress the collective consciousness for the betterment of the earth and all beings on it.

I can almost see Johnny roll his eyes when I profess this. Oh I know it's idealistic, it's dreamlike, it's unimaginable, probably silly, but it's a possibility, why not? Dreamers are the seed planters of the future. I dream and I plant. Everyone does. It's *what* we dream about and decide to plant that matters. And even though manifesting, holding and sharing this high vibration of energy doesn't require having sex, it does require holding a fierce tone of love. And isn't love the only true poetry? And isn't everything sexual at the core?

So I say pleasure *is* my higher calling and I believe it is my noble obligation to heed the call. Johnny can laugh and believe that he needs to fill the tank of a Jaguar first. But I think the reason he stays in touch is because he remembers how it's possible to feel, how he felt when we were generating pleasure together. That energy of pleasure is a free and renewable resource. When Johnny was off the grid, playing with me, his tank never ran out of fuel. Maybe he'll miss that enough to heed the call on his own one day.

I wish that for him and anyone else who wants to experience life with Pleasure as a Higher Calling.

About The Author

Savannah Aries is a sassy, passionate, contemporary woman who claims and advocates *Pleasure as a Higher Calling.* Her spicy stories of life, love, sensuality and lust highlight the adventures of a juicy mature woman, creating, navigating and enjoying the new rules of engagement.

Women (and men!) of all ages are delighting in her humorous perspective, peppered with a bit of well-deserved angst, as she attempts to unravel and make sense of life's most enduring mystery: the luscious story of Love.

Savannah lives in the beautiful Pacific Northwest.

Visit Savannah's author website:

www.savannaharies.com

Like Savannah on Facebook:

http://www.facebook.com/savannah.aries

www.ingramcontent.com/pod-product-compliance
Lightning Source LLC
Chambersburg PA
CBHW020623130626
46552CB00003B/1078